I WANNA TEXT YOU UP

TEAGAN HUNTER

Copyright © 2017 by Teagan Hunter

This book is a work of fiction. Names, characters, businesses, places, events, and incidents are either the products of the author's imagination or used in a fictitious manner. Any resemblance to actual persons, living or dead, or actual events is purely coincidental.

All rights reserved. No part of this publication may be reproduced or transmitted in any form or by any means, electronic or mechanical, including photocopying, recording, or any information storage and retrieval system, without permission in writing from the publisher, except by a reviewer quoting brief passages for review purposes only.

Cover Design by Emily Wittig Designs

Editing by Editing by C. Marie

*To Megan Green, for giving this book the best title ever.
You're my hero. Don't ever change.*

CHAPTER 1

"ARE YOU SURE ABOUT THIS? It seems a bit...sketchy."

"What exactly is so sketchy about it?"

"You're putting up a flyer and inviting strangers into our apartment."

I hold up a finger. "Nuh uh. *You* don't get to have a say in this. You're the one leaving me. This is *my* apartment now."

Delia, my best friend and soon-to-be former roommate, sighs in defeat and crosses her arms over her chest. "Fine. You're right. I just think it's a little...I don't even know. Makes me worried you're going to get some creeper trying to move in with you."

"I promise to vet each one before I make a decision. Sound good?"

She nods. "I'll take what I can get with you."

I adjust the laptop on my knees and lean back into the couch, my gaze planted firmly on the blinking cursor on the nearly blank screen. All I have so far is ROOMMATE WANTED. I'm going to need more than that.

"I still cannot believe you're ditching me to move in with your stupid boyfriend," I tell Delia.

"And goats. Don't forget those sweet baby goats I bought her," said stupid boyfriend interjects, piping up from behind the stack of boxes he's preparing to haul out of the apartment.

"Yeah, what he said." There's a smile on her lips that tells me if I weren't in the room right now, they'd likely not be clothed.

These two lovebirds make me sick.

"Gross, stop smiling at him like that."

He pops his head out, a shit-eating grin covering his face, green eyes lit with mischief. "Did she do that sexy thing where one side of her lips tilts up? God, I love that fucking smile. Talk about a boner inducer."

I throw a disgusted look his way. "Can we not discuss your dick right now, Zach? We're trying to be sad."

"I mean, I guess we don't *have* to. It is a pretty spectacular subject though."

Delia nods. "He isn't wrong."

Groaning, I toss myself back on the couch. "You two are terrible."

"Are we really though, Zoe?"

"Can I kill him now?" I say to Delia.

"No," Zach answers. "I—"

"Zachary Hastings!"

He throws a grin his girlfriend's way, not buying the false reprimand from her either. "I'm going, I'm going."

Stacking up two boxes, he hustles his way from the room before I lob something heavy at his head.

"Are you sure you want to live with him already? You don't think it's too soon?"

She meets my questioning gaze with a serious, sure one of her own. "I'm ready."

I know she is, and that's what makes me so sad. We've been joined at the hip since freshman year. After sharing a dorm room for the last three years, we finally managed to score an apartment off campus last summer for our senior year and beyond. Our friendship, though it was already solid, has grown by leaps and bounds.

She's my person, and I'm going to miss the hell out of her.

"Are *you* ready? For a new roomie, I mean. So soon? That's a big leap, and we both know you don't *need* someone to help foot the bill. Your parents—bless them both—take care of damn near everything already."

"I know, but I think I'm going to get lonely fast. We both know I'm the more social one out of the two of us."

Delia nods. "True, but do you really want to post a flyer? Why don't you just, I don't know, go out?"

I place a hand on my chest and gasp. "Do you mean I should, like, go out and *meet* someone the old-fashioned way?"

She cringes. "No, you're right—people are gross. A flyer works, but *do not* give your personal information! You don't want any randbro to get ahold of that."

"Like the randbro who got ahold of yours? What happened with him again?" I tap my chin, pretending to think.

Delia pushes my hand away. "Stop it. You know what happened."

"Yes, you *banged* him. You banged the first random guy who got ahold of your digits, and now you're moving in with him!"

She rolls her eyes just as Zach walks back into the apartment.

"I'll have you know I had to suffer through three dates with this broad before she finally gave it up. Three. Dates. Do you know how much she cost me in food alone?"

Before I can do it, Delia grabs the nearest pillow off the couch and chucks it Zach's way. "Go away, you ass!"

He dodges the assault and laughs. "You know you love me, my little food whore."

I watch as Delia's eyes light up, the dopiest smile spreading on her face. "I do."

Part of me wants to pretend to puke over their display, but more so, I love the way they love each other.

Nothing was traditional about their courtship—having met via a wrong number—and I don't think either of them would have it any other way. Somehow that wrong number turned into the purest, easiest love I've ever witnessed.

"Get a room," I tease to break the sexual tension building between them.

Zach lifts a shoulder. "I guess we could take her room for a spin one last time."

My mouth drops open and Delia throws her head back in laughter.

"You have no shame, Zach Hastings."

He shrugs again, not the least bit bashful, before grabbing more boxes and leaving.

Delia tucks her feet under her legs and looks my way. "I really will miss you, you know. I can't believe we won't be living together anymore."

"I can't believe you're ditching me, and I can't believe Zach is kicking Robbie out."

"Hey, he's not kicking him out. Robbie left before Zach even asked me to move in."

I barely manage to not roll my eyes. "Oh, puh-lease. Like those boys didn't have it planned. Zach knew you'd say yes. Robbie knew you'd say yes. He bailed for you, Delia. Don't play."

"I know, but if I pretend he didn't then I don't feel as bad."

I laugh at her honesty. "Well he's on to bigger and better things, so that's all that matters."

"You two still talking every day?"

When I first saw Robbie, Zach's best friend and former roommate, during the Great Goat Heist last year, I was immediately attracted to him. I mean, with muscles for days, tattoos, and a killer grin, who could really blame a girl?

But then I learned he's a single father, and I don't do kids. That was the bucket of water on my lust fire, and I knew then we were destined to remain just friends, which, as it turned out, was exactly what we both needed.

While Delia and Zach were off falling in love, we grew close, talking about anything and everything, including my recent mishaps in the dating world and him trying to win back the mother of his child. Now I can't imagine ever being attracted to him. He's my wingman, too much like a big brother to be anything else.

"Yep. He's loving his new place, by the way, said his ex is happy with him for getting out on his own. So, really, don't feel bad about him moving out. It's working out for him."

She nods. "Good. That's good. I just wish I had gotten more time to get to know him, because I'm certain he still thinks I'm halfway insane."

"Only halfway? Are you sure? I mean you *did* climb through his bedroom window last year in an attempt to steal a baby goat."

"But," she begins to argue, "he's also friends with Zach, and he's the looniest of us all."

"Good point."

"Don't worry ladies, you just sit there and cry and whatever else it is you're doing. I'll just handle *all* these heavy boxes myself."

"We will!" Delia tells a passing Zach, his arms stacked

full again. "Anyway, back to the roommate search—if you're sure that's what you want."

I ponder this a moment. Part of me wants to try having the apartment to myself, but I *will* get bored and lonely. I'll succumb to bothering Delia in a heartbeat, and I don't want to be that desperate friend who needs reassurance when the other one gets a boyfriend.

No. I need a new roomie to keep me sane, and entertained.

"I am," I tell her.

She claps her hands together. "Okay, then let's get to work. I'm going to help make you this flyer before I leave."

"Leave?" I balk. "I thought you weren't going until tomorrow? Tonight is supposed to be our last pizza party and sleepover before you ditch me for the pretty boy."

"Chill." She holds her hand out. "We're still having the slumber party, but I want to get started on this now. We want to make sure it's perfectly Zoe."

"What does that mean exactly?"

"You know," she says flippantly.

I cross my arms over my chest, smirking at her. "No, Delia, I don't. Tell me exactly who Zoe is."

"A little edgy. A little sarcastic. Crass. Adorable." She winks at me and I laugh. "I don't know. You're...you. Whoever your new roomie is better like making breakfast to DMX and not be alarmed when you hole up in your room for days on end because you're in the middle of a project."

"Do you think we really need to include all that?"

She shrugs. "Probably not. It does make you sound a bit crazy."

"I feel like I need to make a list. Let me grab my notebook."

I push myself off the couch and make my way down the hall to my bedroom, pausing in front of Delia's nearly empty one. There are only six boxes and her bed left. Other than that, it's bare.

There's a twinge in my heart, and I can feel the tears beginning to form. I try to quickly blink them away. *I will not cry. I will not cry. I will* not *cry, dammit!*

"She's going to miss you, you know."

I jump at the sudden sound and turn to glare at the intruder. "You're a damn ninja, Zach."

He grins. "Sorry." He clearly isn't. "I just wanted you to know that. I feel like I should apologize or feel bad about stealing her away, but I can't."

I pat his shoulder. "And you shouldn't. You two are great together. You deserve this happiness. I'm just annoyed you're stealing my woman. You swooped right in and BAM! Now she's leaving me."

"She'll still come around. I'll make sure of it."

"You make it sound like you're going to have to pry her from your side. I don't think you're *that* great, Zach."

One brow shoots up. "Oh, I beg to differ."

I laugh and push past him. "I'm glad to see your ego is

still intact," I say over my shoulder before turning into my bedroom.

"Hey, I'm just stating the obvious."

I shake my head and grab my worn notebook off my bed before heading back to the living room. I take this thing with me everywhere, and it's evident in the way the cover is beginning to fall off the spiral binding. Maybe it's time I replace it.

I'm a strange breed of people when it comes to notebooks. I use every square inch on a page. Doodles, notes, lists, random reading assignments—it all goes in my book.

"Your boyfriend is so arrogant," I tell Delia, reclaiming my spot next to her then flipping open my notebook and trying to find a blank space to write on.

"Isn't he though? It's kind of exhausting at times."

"Kind of?"

"Okay, a lot. He wears me out, but I totally love it." She sighs again, all wistful-like. "Anyway, let's order that pizza now. I'm starving."

"Is Zach staying for dinner?"

"Oh hell no. I'm not sharing with him. He may call me a food whore all the time, but he's just as bad. He'll scarf the whole thing down before I even get a slice in."

"What a pig."

"I heard that!" Zach says as he makes his way back into the apartment. "I have about two more trips to make and then I'll be out of your hair, ladies. You two can order pizza and gossip and naked pillow fight—you know, the usual things girls do."

I glance to Delia. "He still thinks we naked pillow fight?"

"He won't let it go. He's going to be so disappointed that the only thing we plan to do is scrub this makeup off, ditch the bras, and put on some yoga pants."

"He says you had him at no bras." Zach waggles his brows up and down.

Delia throws another pillow at him and he laughs, taking off to finish up.

He makes three more trips, gives his girl a kiss good-bye, and leaves us to commemorate our last night as roommates.

"Pizza is ordered," I say as Delia trudges back into the living room, her blanket and pillow in hand.

"Fort?" she suggests.

"Like you even had to ask."

We get to work on building a small fort between the couch, coffee table, TV stand, and borrowed stools from the bar in the kitchen.

Once we have everything set up, we snuggle down into our blankets and pull up *Parenthood*, the show we've been binge-watching for weeks now. I'm sad because we still have an entire season to go and she's moving out.

"I still can't believe you're leaving this brand new couch behind for me."

"That was all on Zach. He's the one who insisted on

buying it when Marshmallow chewed one of the cushions, not me. I told him we could just flip it around and not be bothered by it. I have no problems parting with it, and besides, it's not like we'll need it. He does have a fully furnished home, ya know."

She isn't wrong there, and it *was* his goat that chewed up my couch.

"Yeah, yeah, I know—you're moving in with a rich boy who has his shit together."

"He isn't a rich boy," she says defensively. I pin her with a stare. "Okay, he has money, but he isn't a 'rich boy'. That sounds so...dickish."

"Fair enough. Zach isn't a rich boy. He's just...well kept."

Delia snorts out a laugh. "We'll go with that. Pull your laptop over here. Let's get started on that flyer." I push the computer her way. She props it up on her knees, cracking her knuckles and hovering her fingers over the keyboard. "Now, what's the first thing you're looking for in your new roomie?"

"Hmm... Long brown hair. Snarky. Preferably named Delia."

"Such a drama bomb. What are you *really* looking for?"

"I want someone who's going to clean up after themselves. Someone who isn't into parties but is okay with overnight guests...if you catch my drift."

"Obviously. Ladies only?"

"Nah. Chicks or dicks welcome."

Delia chuckles. "That is *so* going on the flyer." She begins typing. "Wait, why aren't we going digital with this? Putting it up on Craigslist or something? You'll reach more potential candidates that way."

I shake my head. "There's something more personal about a flyer, gives it that human touch."

"You sure?"

"What? You don't think it'll be effective?"

"I just find it hard to believe people pay that much attention to bulletin boards anymore."

"Just trust me on this. I'll find someone, and it'll be just the right someone. Now, let's start with this..."

ROOMMATE WANTED
Chicks or dicks welcome!

Looking for a new roomie?
I have a place for you! Like your music loud?
I own headphones.
Enjoy having late-night guests over?
Again, headphones. ;-)
Want someone to help pay the bills?
Do the dishes? Take out the trash?
You scratch my back and I'll scratch yours
(metaphorically, of course).
Check us out, getting along already.

Must be able to pay first
and last month's rent up front.
Must be okay with Breakfast & Beats.
No dogs.
No trying to sleep with me.
Two bedrooms. One bathroom.
$350/month plus electricity.

If interested, email ineedarobin@gmail.com
P.S. Dick pics sent directly to my grandmother.
Don't do that shit to her.

CHAPTER 2

FROM: themredwardnigma@gmail.com

TO: ineedarobin@gmail.com

SUBJECT: I saw your flyer…

Dear Batman,

I'm going to assume, based on your email, you'd like to be addressed as Batman. I'm sort of a comic nerd, so please excuse me if I'm wrong.

Anyway, I saw your flyer on the bulletin board on campus and have a few questions before we seal this deal.

1. What's wrong with the apartment? Is it the location? The condition? That's awfully cheap for the area.

2. You said no dogs—is that no pets or just no dogs?

3. What does the electricity bill typically run?

4. Do you have a move-in date available?

This isn't a question, but I wanted to say you're welcome for not including a dick pic.

Thank you for your time,
Mr. Edward Nigma

FROM: ineedarobin@gmail.com
TO: themredwardnigma@gmail.com
SUBJECT: You got lucky

Dear Edward,

I have to say that including a picture of a COCK and not a DICK...well, that one made me laugh. You earned your reply.

1. Nothing is wrong with the apartment and it's in a nice area. Rent is inexpensive because my parents love me and won't let me work long hours during school. They pay a good portion of the rent.

2. Dogs specifically. I'm not a fan. I'm a cat person. I only recently found out we can have pets and thought I'd include that for when you sign the lease. You know, covering my ass and all that.

3. The electric bill typically runs about $50.

4. The apartment is available immediately, but I would like to take the time to get to know you first before you move in. Possibly two weeks from now? That's not too much to ask, right?

Now that we got that out of the way, tell me about yourself, Edward. Make me want to have you as a roommate.

Best,
The Non-Bruciest of all Bruce Waynes

FROM: themredwardnigma@gmail.com
TO: ineedarobin@gmail.com
SUBJECT: Oh, you want me.

Batman,

Not to sound like a walking cliché, but I'm kind of the ideal roommate. I work and have other obligations, so I don't spend a tremendous amount of time at home. You'll probably be on your own often. I don't party, hardly ever have guests over, and I'm a neat freak. In fact, you'll be so bummed I've moved out when it comes time for me to get a big boy job and leave you behind that you won't know what to do with yourself.

I should also note that you're in luck—I'm a cat person myself. He's six months old and would love to come along to a new place with me. I've included a picture of him in an attempt to charm you.

FROM: ineedarobin@gmail.com
TO: themredwardnigma@gmail.com
SUBJECT: Still on the fence…

Edward,

Though including the picture of the cat was a good idea, I'm still on the fence. You sound too good to be true.

How are we going to fix this? I'm worried about giving up this amazing room to someone who will let me down. Not saying you will but… #trustissues

Also…you're a dude. You have a dick.

I have a vagina.

Will that be an issue?

FROM: themredwardnigma@gmail.com
TO: ineedarobin@gmail.com
SUBJECT: No issues.

Batman,

The apartment sounds too good to be true. Guess we're at an impasse there.

What would you having a vagina change? I'll still have a dick. Are *you* going to be okay living with a guy? Because it's not going to be a problem for me at all.

Is there anything I can do to convince you I'm not a complete shitbag?

FROM: ineedarobin@gmail.com
TO: themredwardnigma@gmail.com
SUBJECT: Hmmm…

Edward,

Send more cat pictures.

FROM: themredwardnigma@gmail.com
TO: ineedarobin@gmail.com
SUBJECT: Easy to please.

Batman,

DONE

P.S. His name is Mittens.

P.P.S. I'm sorry it's taken me a few days to respond.
Remember when I said I work a lot and am rarely home? It's
been one of those weeks. I'm not a flake, I promise.

FROM: ineedarobin@gmail.com
TO: themredwardnigma@gmail.com
SUBJECT: BECAUSE OF HIS PAWS?!

Edward,

I won't lie, I really needed that today.

I only thought you were a flake for about ten minutes until I remembered you said you have a nutso schedule. Where do you work that keeps you so busy, and how do you manage that while in school? And you said you have other obligations on top of all that? What year are you? That sounds like a lot for a college student to take on. Really unfair, if you ask me.

FROM: ineedarobin@gmail.com
TO: themredwardnigma@gmail.com
SUBJECT: Apologies

Edward,

It's been two days since I've heard from you.

Either you're busy or you think I'm a nosy, judgmental brat.

I apologize if I overstepped any boundaries. I promise I'm not usually so…obnoxious.

You seem like a cool guy and I hope I didn't ruin anything.

P.S. I really only want you to be my roommate so I can pet your…cat.

FROM: themredwardnigma@gmail.com
TO: ineedarobin@gmail.com
SUBJECT: Ugh.

Batman,

I knew it was only about the cat.

Your questions weren't too intrusive. I'm a senior and keep busy with working the graveyard shift, sports, and family obligations.

Honestly, I don't know how I do it all either. It's kind of a lot, but someone's gotta do it, right? At least that's what I keep telling myself. If I'm not taking care of things, who will?

Anyway, I'm rambling now. You don't need to hear any of this.

Keep me updated on the availability, please.

FROM: ineedarobin@gmail.com
TO: themredwardnigma@gmail.com
SUBJECT: I understand

Edward,

I can understand where you're coming from. I'm an only child and admittedly I've lived a good life, but I'm sort of a perfectionist.

Being a perfectionist and an artist *don't* go hand in hand.

I know, I know, I do it to myself, but I can't help it. My brain won't let me move on until things are *just right*…but then I feel like nothing is ever just right.

Hence my dating life and less than stellar track record there.

Ugh, now *I'm* the one rambling. You really don't need to hear all of this.

The apartment is still available. I've had a few others email, but nothing has felt right. Not even you.

Wow, this whole thing just came full circle, didn't it?

I'm stopping before I tell you my entire life story—no one wants to hear that.

FROM: themredwardnigma@gmail.com
TO: ineedarobin@gmail.com
SUBJECT: For what it's worth, I'm a good listener.

Batman,

Brace yourself…hard-hitting question coming in 3, 2, 1…

Do you think I'm roommate material? I've run into some… well, let's say issues, and I sort of need to get the ball rolling on finding a cheaper place to live. I looked at apartments on my day off yesterday and every one I saw was either infested with mice, had bongs scattered about (which, hey, whatever floats your boat), or the renter greeted me in their underwear. As you can see, the conditions weren't ideal. Your place just *sounds* much nicer than these.

Do I have a shot? Or should I keep looking?

FROM: ineedarobin@gmail.com
TO: themredwardnigma@gmail.com
SUBJECT: Desperate

Edward,

The reason it's taken me two days to respond is…

You sound desperate, and slightly shady.

Half of me is like "oh man this poor dude," but the other half
—the cautious half—is saying you sound *too* desperate, and
that means you're going to turn out to be a creeper or a
murderer.

To fix this, I think we need to meet…in a very public setting.
Then I can decide if you're a creeper or not.

Thoughts? Opinions? Concerns?

FROM: themredwardnigma@gmail.com
TO: ineedarobin@gmail.com
SUBJECT: Deal

Batman,

I'm in.

Lola's on Tuesday at 6PM okay?

FROM: ineedarobin@gmail.com
TO: themredwardnigma@gmail.com
SUBJECT: RE: Deal

Edward,

It's a date!

FROM: ineedarobin@gmail.com
TO: themredwardnigma@gmail.com
SUBJECT: WTF

I DID NOT MEAN A *DATE* DATE.

Because there will be no bangin', remember? No trying to stick your magic wang into this hot pocket.

GOT IT?

FROM: themredwardnigma@gmail.com

TO: ineedarobin@gmail.com

SUBJECT: GOT IT

You mean I can't put my Lik-A-Stix in your Fun Dip? Open the gates of Mordor with Gandalf's staff? Slytherin to your Chamber of Secrets? Put my email in your spam folder?

Wow. Why don't you just take *all* the fun out of this then?

P.S. YEAH, I GOT IT.

CHAPTER 3

"HOW ARE you supposed to know which one is him?"

"Ah, shit," I mutter under my breath. "We didn't talk about this. I've been so scatterbrained this week trying to make the deadline on my project that I didn't even think to ask. Crap."

It's been just under two weeks since Edward contacted me about the empty room I have, and my first reaction to him was laughing at his name.

Edward? How *Twilight*.

Then I laughed at what he sent me—a picture of a rooster—because, hey, it wasn't a dick pic. I knew right then I had to email him back, and he was the frontrunner in my search. He's the *exact* kind of roommate I'd like to have.

"Are you sure about this, Zoe? I mean, he sounded desperate for the room. That should be a red flag, right?"

I nod. "It should be, but it didn't *feel* like one—know what I mean?"

She twists her lips up and I know she agrees with me. I showed her every email Edward sent. Neither of us felt anything off about him, though we felt we should because of his neediness.

I watch as she pushes her sunglasses up on her nose and laughs. Delia insisted she be here for the meet and greet but didn't want to be *that* friend. So, instead, she's sitting on the other side of the bar, wearing head-to-toe black, and Zach is here too, wearing a black ball cap pulled low over his eyes, a hoodie with the hood pulled up, and jeans.

They stick out like sore thumbs.

"You two look like idiots," I tell her.

"Shut up," she growls as she flips me off. Zach catches wind of what she's doing and flips the bird my way too, not even knowing why.

He's such a good support system.

"Do you think he's here already?" I hear Zach ask her.

"I don't see anyone who looks like an Edward."

"And how does one look like an Edward?" Zach asks. I can hear the smile in his voice. "Pale and constipated looking?"

Delia gasps and smacks at his arm. "How dare you! He was trying to resist her *scent*!"

"Can we please stop discussing *Twilight* and get back to the task at hand? Scan the room with me, Delia. Who looks like he could be my Edward?"

"What about that guy in the corner wearing the tweed jacket? Or the guy in the blue sweater?"

"So, basically the two dudes who are wearing outfits similar to what Edward wore in the movie?"

She opens her mouth but hesitates. "Y-Yes," she finally says.

"You're horrible at this."

"Are you two really talking on the phone across the bar right now?"

I jump at the familiar voice, bumping my drink and sloshing soda onto the table.

I look up at the offender and glare. "You owe me a new Cheerwine."

Caleb Mills smirks down at my delicious cherry-flavored soda. "Cheerwine? Really, Zoe?"

"What? It's a damn good drink and you know it." He nods and slides himself onto a barstool. "Sure, please, take a seat at my table, Caleb."

"Aw, thanks. It *is* a good drink, but you're in a bar— why aren't you drinking?"

I shake my cup at him. "I am."

"What's Caleb doing here?" Delia asks in my ear.

"Hell if I know," I answer her.

Caleb turns around and waves her way. She and Zach both raise their drinks to him.

It still blows my mind how chill Delia and Caleb are after having dated for six months last year. They split amicably with no bad blood between them, but it's *always* awkward when your ex starts dating someone new and you're there to witness it.

Not with them.

Last year after a nude photo of Delia went around, Caleb was right there on the battlefield along with us, making sure to keep the identity of the girl in the photo under wraps and ensuring that the douchebag who sent it got what was coming to him.

That was the first time I noticed him in a way I shouldn't, and it wasn't even in an *omg he's hot* sort of way —I noticed that *long* ago.

No, it was the way he was there fighting for his friend, the way he went against the most powerful player on his team knowing he was putting his career in jeopardy to do the right thing.

It was his fierceness and determination.

His loyalty.

I've been spurned by lack of loyalty far too many times. Caleb's loyalty calls to me, makes me want to get to know him, to get close to him.

I could use someone like him in my life.

"Make him leave. We're on a mission here, Zoe."

"I can't just tell him to go away, Delia. That's rude."

My surprise guest raises a brow. "That *is* rude." He grins, and I consider how cute his grin is.

I'm not blind; I've noticed Caleb before. Hell, I noticed him *well* before Delia ever did, and I've always thought he was attractive in your typical boy-next-door sort of way.

With blond hair that curls at the collar and dark blue

eyes that always have a twinkle in them, Caleb's hand-some, and I've been heartbroken by too many pretty faces in my life.

"Tell him he's the one being rude. Tell him about our mission."

"We're doing something here, Caleb. Do you mind?"

He holds a hand to his chest, that twinkle of his ever present. "Am I that unworthy of your time? Am I so unwelcome after all I've done for you and Delia?"

"Tell that asshat he can only play that card for so long," Delia says.

"I'm not telling him that. He has a point."

"Point, schmoint." She pulls the phone from her mouth. "Hey, we're working here!" she shouts with an accent. I'm certain she was aiming for New Jersey, but it's not even close to actually sounding like that.

Caleb laughs and shakes his head. "Cheerwine, right?"

I nod and he takes off, heading toward the bar.

"What did you say this guy's name was again?" I hear Zach ask Delia.

"Edward Cullen," she replies.

"His name is *not* Edward Cullen, you ass!" I hiss through the phone.

"Fine. Just Edward."

"What was his email address again?"

"You showed him the emails?" It comes out as a screech, and the patrons occupying the table next to mine look my way. I give them a look, and they all turn their attention away.

"What? I needed his opinion too."

"That was *private* information, Delia!"

"It's just Zach. Big whoop."

"Just Zach," I hear him say, a hint of sarcasm in his voice. "Zoe, what was his email address?"

"I don't know!" Caleb slides a new Cheerwine in front of me and I nod my thanks to him as he takes a seat. "Look it up."

I wait as Zach and Delia scroll through her phone in an attempt to find the emails I forwarded her.

Watching as Caleb takes a swig of his beer, I can't help but be mesmerized by the way he swallows...which is the dumbest thing I've ever been enthralled by.

I'm not surprised by it though.

Ever since Caleb showed his white knight side, my eyes have slid his way more than once. My interest is officially piqued.

But it can't be.

He's my best friend's ex-boyfriend, for fuck's sake. That *can't* happen. It's girl code rule one—you don't date or sleep with someone your best friend did.

Which means I can't notice his indigo eyes or the way they crinkle at the edges when he smiles, can't be drawn to the stupid dimple in his chin or that ridge on his nose indicating it's been broken a time or two, and there's no reason

I should want to lick away the drop of beer clinging to his full lips.

But, I do.

Shit.

I shake my head and focus back in on the conversation between Delia and Zach.

"You guys find anything out of the ordinary?"

"Aha! Got it!" Delia says. "Give Zach a moment."

I watch him swipe his finger over the screen, scrolling through our emails and scanning them quickly.

"How did you miss this, Zoe? It's obvious as hell."

"Miss what?" I ask, half interested, half wondering why Caleb's right hand is in a brace.

I give him a kick under the table, catch his eye, and nod toward it.

"Fracture," he mutters. My eyes widen, worried because I know what that could mean for his baseball career. "It's fine."

Those midnight eyes of his say differently, but I let it go. I nod and tune back in to Zach. "—ame. Did you hear me, Zoe?"

"No. Repeat that."

"Edward is not his name. He was playing off your email address and acting as a comic book character too."

"What? Who? Which one?"

"The Riddler, whose real name is Edward Nigma. E. Nigma. *Enigma.* Get it?"

I nod at him, processing what he's telling me. That

means I know nothing of substance about the guy I'm meeting tonight, not even his name.

Crap.

What was I thinking doing this? Inviting a stranger to live with me? I must be insane.

"Are you sure, Zach?"

"You're asking me, the king nerd, if I'm sure? Yes, I'm positive."

"So what—or who—should I be looking for here?"

He chuckles at the irritation lining my voice, and I want so badly to flip him the bird. "Probably someone with a riddle on his shirt."

"I don't..." I glance around the bar, trying to read the t-shirt of every guy sitting alone. There's one I can't make out from here, and I know Zach and Delia won't be able to read it either. "Hold on, let me check this dude out."

I hop off the barstool and march toward the guy. He's sipping on a soda, and when he catches me moving toward him, he sits up straight, pushing his glasses up on his nose.

His shirt isn't much of a riddle, just one of those picture plus picture equals whatever kind of things. It's riddle enough for me.

I plant myself directly in front of him, brow raised. "You him?"

He glances around, eyes nervous as he wraps a hand around his drink. He takes a sip through the straw before sucking in a breath. "M-Mistress Jasmine?"

My eyes widen, and his cheeks turn pink as he ducks his head, mortified.

I guess neither of us are who we thought we were.

"My bad. Wrong guy," I mutter before retreating back to my table, Delia and Zach laughing in my ear.

"Shut up," I bark at them.

"I didn't even say a word," Caleb says, hands raised in innocence, not the least bit troubled by my abrupt exit and return.

I throw him a look and he smirks, knowing he's being a smartass.

"Anything else he'd be wearing, Zach?"

"Maybe a question mark? That's a signature Riddler thing. I'd hope he wouldn't be so cliché though."

"We don't need your nerd snobbery right now, Mr. Hastings."

He tsks in my ear. "Hey, I'm just saying, you ladies really should have included me in this. I could have been way more inventive than Robin, Batman, and the Ridd— ow!" Delia gives his shin a kick, and I want to high-five her for having my back. "Amateurs," he mutters.

My eyes scroll across the bar, looking for anyone wearing something with a question mark on it. I peek at the loner guys again, but none of them are fitting the criteria.

"Do you guys see anyone?"

Both answer in the negative.

"Maybe he isn't here yet?" Delia suggests. "I mean we did get here five minutes early."

"Yes, and now he'd be five minutes late."

"Who are you guys looking for?" Caleb interjects.

"We aren't su—" My eyes trail over Caleb's shirt and my breath catches in my throat. "No."

"What?"

My gaze stays trained on the pocket of his shirt. I can't look away, because right there in plain sight sits a question mark, peeping out at the top of the square.

Without thought, I reach over and pull his pocket down, the beer that was halfway to his lips sloshing out of the glass with the sudden jerking movement.

I was right.

Sitting inside his pocket is the Riddler, arms stretched wide in a *Here I am!* gesture.

Caleb's head snaps my way, his own dark blue gaze wide, surprise covering his face.

"No." The word drops from his lips in a whisper. "There is no way."

"I'll call you back," I say before ending the call and setting my phone on the table, never once breaking eye contact with Caleb.

"You're the one I've been emailing with?" he says, voice full of surprise.

"You're the one I was going to let move in with me?"

"I guess I—wait, *was?* Past tense?"

His nostrils flare with irritation as my words sink in,

and God help me, I find it attractive. I don't know what is up with me tonight, but I'm noticing things in Caleb I shouldn't be.

Ugh.

"Past tense."

"Why, Zoe? Why can't we be roommates? We know each other. I'd say we're comfortable enough around each other, and you don't have to be worried about letting some stranger danger move in. This is the perfect setup here."

I shake my head. "No. No way."

"Why? Give me one good reason why not."

"Because you're my best friend's ex-boyfriend, that's why." *And because I find you extremely attractive, idiot.*

With how much I've been noticing him lately, there is no way in hell I can confine myself to an apartment with the guy. That's a recipe for disaster and too many late-night *me time* sessions.

He sighs and scrubs a hand over his face. "Who gives a crap about that? It feels like a lifetime ago. She's moved on, *I've* moved on—that's not a real reason."

"It's reason enough for me."

"And if I were to march over there right now and ask Delia if it was okay and she said yes, then what?"

"Then the answer would still be no. It's *my* apartment."

He lets out an exasperated sigh and his shoulders slump. I almost feel bad for telling him no, but I can't say yes. It'd be too weird knowing he'd just been sleeping there as Delia's boyfriend less than a year ago.

"Zoe..." My name comes out as a plea, and my resolve begins to waver.

"Why? Why do you need it so badly? I thought you had a place already."

"I do, but I need something cheaper. I... Fuck, I screwed up, okay? I got into a...scuffle. Yeah, let's call it a scuffle. I messed my hand up pretty damn bad." He holds up said hand to show me the brace again. "Anyway, my medical bills are going to start stacking up and I can't risk them taking over my budget. I was already looking for something cheaper because my hours got cut, but when I add this on top of it...yeah. I *need* this, Zoe. You have no idea how bad either. *Please.*"

I can hear the desperation in his voice, and a part of me wants to say yes, but hesitation is still winning. I don't want things to turn awkward, and I think they will. I mean, how does one *live* with their best friend's ex-boyfriend? When it hasn't even been a year since the breakup? When he's stupid attractive?

I cast one last glance his way, the look in his eyes giving me pause. They're tired and sad and needy all at once. I don't know what to do with that.

Studying his face, I notice he's worn down beyond the normal senior-year-coming-to-an-end fatigue.

He's emotionally and mentally drained, and he desperately needs to catch a break.

I can't turn him away, not right now. I just need to pull my big girl panties up—and keep them pulled up—and offer him my spare room like any good friend would do.

"Do you really have a pet cat?"

"Why would I lie about that?"

Shrugging, I say, "Who knows. People are weird."

"Yes, Mittens is real."

"Ask Delia," I concede.

"Are you sure?"

I nod. "I'm sure, but Delia *has* to be okay with it."

Just like that, he sits up a little straighter, eyes shining a little brighter.

Maybe this won't be so bad after all.

CHAPTER 4

"ARE YOU SURE ABOUT THIS?"

"You keep asking me that, I'm going to change my mind."

"I just want to be sure, Zoe. You seem reluctant about this whole thing."

"That's because I am."

"Am I really that bad?"

I look at him for the first time since I pulled into his rather questionable-looking apartment complex. For someone who's been living here for the last four years, he doesn't have a lot. His entire bedroom fits inside my SUV since they wouldn't let him bring his mattress along, claiming it was theirs first and not his.

Some roommates, huh?

The truth is, he's *not* that bad, and that's part of the problem.

In fact, Caleb isn't bad at all. He's...hot, especially with his ball cap twisted around on his head, leather jacket covering broad shoulders.

But that's the last thing I need to be thinking about. Instead, I focus on loading the last of his boxes, most of which are full of bagged and boarded comic books, trying to take the brunt of the work with his hand in the condition it is. I never knew Caleb was such a comic lover. It's kind of...cute, in a nerdy sort of way.

"No, Caleb, you're not bad. It's just...weird. You're Delia's ex-boyfriend."

His eyes fall to slits. "Yes, you keep reminding me of that as if I'm not the one who dated her for six months. Why exactly is that so weird for you? It's not like we hung out a lot or anything, just a group movie here and there."

I don't know *why* I keep reminding him.

Is it because no one will ever match up to Delia and I'm still hurt by her moving? Possibly.

Or could it be because I have a sinking feeling in my gut that with Caleb and me living in such close quarters, those stupid feelings I've developed toward him are going to grow into something more? Even more possible.

Ignoring him, I push the box I'm holding farther into the back, bending to grab another from the concrete to keep busy.

Moving too fast, my head starts swimming and I sway, crashing into Caleb. He reaches out to steady me and my skin feels like it's on fire the moment he makes contact, so hot I inhale a sharp breath.

He doesn't miss it.

My hazel eyes collide with his dark blue gaze. There's a lighter blue seeping into the outer rim of his irises that I've never noticed before. I inch closer, wanting a better look. I'm so close I can feel his breath ghosting on my lips. There's an errant hair sticking out of his cap that I so badly want to brush away.

Caleb's pupils dilate and his gaze flits to my lips, lingering there for far too long.

He wants to kiss me. He wants to kiss me *bad*.

I snap myself out of my lustful state because I *cannot* let that happen, and by the way he inches back, he knows it too.

"Holy crap—*that's* why you don't want me to live with you." He grins, and it's full of playfulness for the first time since I pulled up. "You want me."

"I want you...to stop touching me and help me get this shit loaded up." I pull out of his grasp completely and haul another box into my car. "We're burning daylight here."

"It's two in the afternoon—how long do you think it'll take us to get this into our new place?"

I lift a brow his way. "*Our* new place?"

"Hey, I signed that line, so that's *my* apartment now too."

"You don't even pay half the rent. It's still my apartment."

It takes me a moment to realize he's stopped loading. I stand up straight and meet his gaze.

That lustful stare he was just giving me? Gone. In its place is an icy glower.

Folding my arms across my chest, I let out an exasperated sigh. "What, Caleb?"

"Is this how it's going to be? It's *your* place and nothing is mine? I just have a room there and that's it?"

I regard him with a stony stare of my own. "No."

He doesn't budge, not buying it.

Hell, *I'm* not buying it. It's not his fault I'm sexually frustrated and want to jump his bones. I shouldn't take it out on him.

I sigh and throw my hands up in defeat. "No, Caleb, that's not how it's going to be, okay? I'm just being cranky. I promise it won't be like that."

"*Promise* promise?"

I grit my teeth together and push out the words. "*Promise* promise."

He beams at me. "Perfect."

We load another box each and then something hits me.

"How are you going to drive your motorcycle with your brace on?" I ask him.

"Carefully...very carefully. I think I can grip the handlebars enough that I don't fall over."

"How'd you get to Lola's?"

"A cab."

"Caleb, this doesn't sound safe. Just ride with me and we'll come back to get your bike later."

He holds his hand up. "How later? Because I'm going to be in this thing for some time."

"Can someone else drive it maybe? I'd rather you *and* the bike make it to the apartment safely."

"I don't want anyone else to drive my precious."

"Caleb."

"Zoe." He huffs. "Fine. We'll leave it here then. I'll see if one of the guys from the team can drive it."

"Or Zach."

"I am *not* asking my ex-girlfriend's boyfriend to drive my motorcycle for me. Now *that* is weird."

"What about my friend Robbie? He rides and I trust him with my life. He'd never let your *precious* get hurt."

"I'll think about it," he bites out, annoyed again.

I stand by as he bends to grab another box, taking his distraction as an opportunity to scroll my eyes over his body...to admire the way his arms flex as he lifts the last container...to soak in the way his shirt clings to his muscled back as he crams the boxes into the hatch.

He begins to twist my way, and I can't pull my eyes away fast enough.

"I think that's the last of it, right?"

"Yep." My voice comes out a squeak and his brow hitches at the sound.

"Right." He closes the hatch. "So we ready then?"

"Yep!"

Another high-pitched squeal.

"You okay?"

"Yep!"

He laughs and bends to grab his helmet, stashing it in the back seat, and I check out his ass.

That tight, perfectly sculpted ass his faded Levi's are hugging in *all* the right places.

I have no fucking shame.

"Try not to jostle everything around too much. I have a couple collectibles in here I'd like to keep in one piece, and don't forget that Mittens is in his carrier. He'll probably cry for a bit and then settle down."

I snap my eyes to his, certain he knows exactly what I was just doing.

For some completely unknown reason, I shoot him two thumbs up. "Yep."

We climb into the car, and that's the moment I realize having him ride with me was a big mistake.

His body fills the car with a sweaty, rugged scent. I hate it and love it all at once.

I shift the car into the drive and start our journey. Mittens lets out a soft meow and Caleb reaches into the back, trying to soothe the kitten, but it's no use. His meows grow louder, his uncertainty about the moving vehicle rising.

"Do you mind if I let him out?"

"Not at all."

I try to keep my focus on the road as he scoops the skittish kitten from his traveling case and snuggles him close to his chest.

You know those silly videos you see online with the hot guys playing with kittens? The big, macho dudes falling apart at the sight of them?

That's what's happening right now, in this car, *right in front of me*—and it's every bit as swoon-worthy as it is in video form.

It's not just about how stupid sexy it is to see him fawning all over Mittens. It's his smile, the way his entire face is lighting up, the way his shoulders relax from their rigid posture.

Looks like Caleb needs Mittens just as much as Mittens needs him.

And maybe I need them both.

"YOU'RE OUT OF SOAP."

Caleb's lived here for all of five hours and I'm already regretting my decision to allow him to move in. I could strangle Delia for saying yes too. He's already used the last of the paper towels, and now my body wash is gone too. Why he wants to smell like Brown Sugar Pears is beyond me.

I groan. "Did you *really* use my body wash?"

"I'm out. I didn't think it'd be a big deal."

Spinning around in my spot on the couch to face him, I let out a shriek when I see he's wearing nothing but a towel.

"Why are you *naked?*"

"I'm not *naked*, Zoe. I have a towel on. Why are you *still* staring at me?"

His lips tilt up and I realize he's right. I *am* still staring, but I can't pull my eyes away now, not when his perfectly sculpted chest is on full display.

You can tell taking care of his body is important to Caleb. You can also tell he spends a lot of his free time at the gym. His biceps are chiseled in just the right way, forearms strong and sturdy, and he's given a little extra attention to his abs, the delectable V guys have drawing my eyes.

There's a water droplet slowly making its way down, down, down beneath the towel. *God do I want to see what's beneath it.*

"Zoe?"

His voice snaps me out of my haze and I bring my eyes to his, cheeks heating with the thoughts racing through my mind.

I will not find my roommate attractive. I will not find my roommate attractive.

"Go put some clothes on, Caleb."

He smirks. "Because you're afraid you're going to try to jump my bones?"

Yes. "No."

"Are you lying?"

Yes. "No."

His smirk grows, because he knows I'm lying, but he doesn't call me on my shit.

Instead he spins around and hustles back down the hallway to his bedroom, only to emerge moments later wearing a plain black t-shirt, gray sweatpants, and no socks.

This might be worse.

There's something so sexy about a guy in sweats with bare feet. It reminds me of a rainy Sunday afternoon spent in bed...which is exactly where I'd like to be right now.

I watch as he makes his way into the kitchen, opening every cabinet there is and closing each one with a thud louder than the last.

When he makes it to the refrigerator, he all-out huffs in disdain.

"Is there *anything* to eat here?"

I lift myself off the couch and take a seat at the bar. "What do you mean? The cabinets are full and there's milk in the fridge."

"There's milk for macaroni and cereal, which is nearly all there is in the cabinets."

"Okay." I draw the word out, confused. "That's food."

He groans. "That's not *real* food."

"It keeps me alive."

"But not healthy."

I roll my eyes. "Boring."

"Smart."

"Then what am I supposed to eat, huh? I can't cook."

His mouth drops open. "You can't cook? Like, at all?"

"I can make eggs and bake...does that count?"

He drops his head into his hands, laughing. "You can cook the one thing I *can't* cook."

"Wait, you can't make eggs? But they're so *easy*."

"Well not for me apparently. What can you bake?"

"Anything."

"Cookies?"

I wave my hand. "Easy."

"Cupcakes? From scratch?"

"That's insulting."

"How about this: you make desserts and I'll make dinners."

"Like...all dinners?"

"All dinners when we're both home," he says. "Except on Sundays. I won't be here on Sundays."

"What happens on Sundays?"

"I have plans."

"Plans?" He nods. "Every single Sunday?" He nods again.

Interesting...

"Do we have a deal then?"

"Deal," I agree.

"Good." He claps his hands together. "We need to shop then."

I hold up a hand. "Starting *now*? I just went shopping two days ago."

"And your cabinets are filled with nothing but junk."

"It's not *that* bad."

"It's pretty bad."

"Fine." I let out a defeated sigh. "Let's go shopping then. I'll put on a proper shirt."

"And pants. Don't forget to put pants on."

"Leggings are pants!" I holler over my shoulder as I make my way into my bedroom.

I listen as Caleb shuffles after me and hear his dresser drawers open. I never hear the bedroom door close and itch to sneak into the hallway to see what I can catch a glimpse of.

Instead I dutifully pull out a t-shirt that isn't three sizes too big, put the plain navy V-neck on, throw my hair into a messy bun, and swipe on a layer of lip gloss.

Caleb saunters out of his room wearing a pair of low-slung jeans instead of the sweatpants he had on, not having bothered to change his shirt. That same ball cap from earlier is backward on his head again, his dark blond hair spilling out from underneath.

I've never understood the appeal of ball caps before. They've always been an odd choice of accessory to me.

Until now.

I don't know if it's the way he's wearing it or if it's that extra swagger it gives him, but *damn*.

Caleb without the cap is cute. Caleb with the cap? *Sexy*.

"You good with driving?"

I jingle my keys. "Yep."

"Mittens was making his way into your room when I walked by—is that okay?"

"Sure, but don't be surprised when he falls in love with me and only wants to sleep in there."

"Ha. Like that will happen."

"Hey, I'm just saying, I'm irresistible."

"You mean irritating."

I glower his way. "Watch it, mister."

He reaches out and tweaks my nose, and I swat his hand away. "You look terrifying. Now scoot. Let's get this show on the road."

We make our way from the apartment and I lock the door behind us. It's a quiet walk to the car but I can feel the heat radiating off his body as he follows me down the sidewalk.

"Where to?" I ask as we click our seatbelts into place.

"You good with Smart Shoppe?"

"Though I am irritated by their use of two Ps and an E, that works. Nice and cheap, just the way I like it."

"I never understood the extra letters either. I think they were just trying to be fancy."

"Those fake fancy bastards." I tsk, turning from the apartment lot and onto the main drag.

The drive is quick and before I know it, Caleb's grabbing a cart and navigating us to the fresh produce section.

"What veggies do you like?" he asks, grabbing a handful of fresh green beans and tossing them into a bag.

"Anything that isn't green."

"Seriously?"

I shrug. "What? It's a gross-looking color."

"How can a *color* be gross-looking?"

"It just can."

He tries his hardest to hold in his sigh, but it's no use. "Fine. Grab what you'll eat then."

I load up on carrots, cauliflower, red potatoes, and butternut squash.

"You like *all* that stuff?"

I blink at him. "Yes. Is that a problem?"

"No, I'm just surprised based on what I found in your cabinets."

"Just because I can half-ass my way through mac and cheese doesn't mean that's all I eat." He stares at me, unmoving. "I order out sometimes too."

A grin breaks out on his face. "I knew that was coming."

"Did you now? You a mind reader?"

"Nope. You're just predictable."

I grab the nearest item and chuck it his way.

"Did you just...did you just throw a fucking potato at me? In the middle of the store?"

I cross my arms over my chest and stare him down. "How's that for predictable?"

He laughs and shakes his head. "You're something else, Zoe."

"Thank you...I think."

"You're welcome. Let's keep moving. I'm starving, and the worst time to grocery shop is when you're hungry."

We move through the store and argue about what to buy.

"Oreos?" I suggest.

"No."

"Pop-Tarts?"

His lips curl at the suggestion. "Negative. How is it you survive off that crap?"

"It's not *that* bad."

"There are no nutrients in them."

"I'll have you know Oreos are *vegan*. There has to be some benefit to them," I try to reason.

"That's not how that works."

"You're not how that works," I mutter.

"I heard that." He grabs a box of whole-wheat noodles and tosses them in the cart.

"Those things taste like cardboard."

"You eat a lot of cardboard in your life?"

He doesn't even bother to turn to look at me, so he doesn't see me flip him off.

"Stop flipping me off."

How in the... "I think I hate you."

"You wish you hated me."

And I wish I didn't want to pull that ball cap from your head and press my lips to yours. Why in the hell does he look so sexy grocery shopping?

Another box of noodles into the cart. "What is Breakfast and Beats?"

"What?"

He gives me a peek over his shoulder before grabbing a jar of organic, sugar-free tomato sauce. "On your flyer you mentioned something called Breakfast and Beats. What is that?"

"Oh." I shrug. "I just like listening to 90s and early 2000s rap music when I make breakfast."

"Eggs, right?"

"Or cereal."

"Cereal isn't real breakfast."

"You're very opinionated about what I'm putting in my mouth."

His eyebrows shoot up and his lips quirk into a twisted smirk as I realize what I just said.

"Oh god, I didn't mean dicks, Caleb. I meant food."

There's a strangled laugh and I turn to find an old lady standing directly behind me. Her hair is a wild mess of white, nails painted blood red, and a cubic zirconia bracelet hangs off her wrist as she grabs for a box of pasta. A long black cover drapes her shoulders, she's wearing skinny black slacks and a white blouse, and a string of knockoff pearls sits around her slender neck to complete her look. She's dressed to the nines, and it's a bit much for Smart Shoppe, especially at this time of night.

My cheeks heat and Caleb doubles over in laughter, having known full well she was standing behind me the entire time. I swat at his bent form, trying to get him to shut up.

"You!" I whack him on the back. "You are such an ass!"

"Oh honey, now don't be embarrassed. There's no shame in taking a little bob on the knob."

She winks and then sashays away, leaving me standing there with my mouth dropped open in shock and a laughing Caleb still by my side.

"Did she just…"

"Yep."

"Holy hell," I murmur.

Caleb stands and wipes at the tears running down his cheeks.

"I think I love that old broad."

"I think *I* love that old broad. I want to be her when I grow up."

Caleb grabs my arms and tugs me down the aisle. "Come on before you run after her and propose marriage."

I try to stick a few more snacks into the cart but it's no use; Caleb notices. After the sixth failed attempt, I give up and let him get whatever he wants.

"So how'd you learn to cook?" I ask as I slip a carton of chocolate milk into the cart.

"I didn't have the option to not learn." He checks the carton of eggs he's holding before handing them my way. "I was the oldest kid and my mom wasn't home often. You can only do so much with mac and cheese and ramen before it gets old."

"That's why I order out from time to time—breaks up the monotony."

He chuckles. "How do you know how to bake but not cook? That seems a bit strange to me."

"Not really, when you think about it. There are a lot of variables to cooking. Baking is simple. There are ingredients that go together to make this or that and you need to bake it for X amount of time. It's all very set in stone, no real room to deviate. I like the rules behind it."

"Hmm...I never thought of it like that."

And that's all he says.

We mosey our way up and down more aisles, arms sliding against one another every so often. I don't know if it's intentional or not, but it's starting to feel like it is. I mean, there are only so many times it can happen accidentally before someone takes notice.

"I'm going to grab a bag or two of frozen fruit for smoothies. You head over and grab a couple bags of steamable veggies you'll eat."

"Roger that."

We head our opposite directions and I survey the coolers, trying to find just what I'm looking for. *Of course* it's on the top shelf, where I'm too short to reach.

I open the door, the cool air hitting me and sending chills down my back, and hoist myself up onto the bottom of the frame. Even standing on my tiptoes, I can't reach the bag of corn. It's sitting at the back of the freezer, just out of reach, even with the boost.

A blanket of heat slides over my back and I shiver again, my nipples coming to peaks. This time it's not from the cool air but the sudden change in temperature.

"Here," Caleb says, his gravelly voice slipping over me, curling into my skin. "Let me get it."

His hand rests on the small of my back, a slight pressure to the touch, and for a moment, neither of us moves. He's so close that I can feel his chest brushing against my ass with every harsh breath he takes.

Our closeness is affecting him too.

I don't know whether to be excited or alarmed by that.

Part of me wants to fall back, see if he'll catch me, wants to know what it would feel like in his arms.

But I don't.

Instead I climb down, savoring the feel of his calloused hand through my thin shirt.

I stand back as Caleb easily reaches up and grabs the bag of corn, tossing it into the basket.

"Anything else?" he asks.

I shake my head, not trusting my voice at this point.

"All right then." He peers into the cart and around at the shelves one last time. "I think we're good here. It's a decent start at stocking up the fridge."

"A decent start? You bought like two of everything."

"And not a single box of mac and cheese."

"But only because we have enough at home, right?"

He shakes his head, amused. "Sure. Now let's check

out before I think on it too much and make you put that chocolate milk back."

"You caught that, huh?"

"You'd make a horrible thief. You're not the least bit slick or subtle."

"Don't be insulting, Caleb."

He rolls his eyes as he pushes the cart up to the belt and begins loading the groceries. "Honest, Zoe—I was being honest."

"Are you always so sassy?"

"Do you always have to have the last word?"

"No."

"You sure?"

"No."

The cashier, a high school student who looks bored out of his mind, pushes the groceries through the scanner and down to the bag boy, who looks just as enthusiastic as our cashier.

"Paper or plastic?" he asks in a monotone voice.

"Paper," Caleb says at the same time I say, "Plastic."

"Paper is better, sturdier."

"I use the plastic bags."

"Mittens uses the paper bags."

"Paper or plastic?" the kid says again.

Caleb and I stare one another down, not wanting to let the other win.

The moment I open my mouth, he does too.

"PAPER!" he shouts at the poor kid, making him jump. Then he throws a cocky grin my way.

I groan and continue loading the belt.

A few minutes and eighty dollars later, we're caught at another stalemate.

"I'm paying."

"No way. I got this."

"Caleb."

"Zoe."

"Just let me get this. You've already spent enough this week with rent."

"No way. Go put the cart up."

"You're being stubborn!" I tell him.

He swipes his debit card. "That's funny coming from you."

"Fine, but we're getting French fries on the way home, just so you know."

"But the groceries..."

"Will be fine for ten minutes or so. Now hurry up so my chocolate milk doesn't go bad."

CHAPTER 5

"THIS WAS the best idea you've had since you let me move in."

Caleb moans as he takes another bite of his burger, swallows, and shoves a handful of fries into his mouth.

I watch every movement with rapt attention.

"Are you making love to that thing or eating it?"

He side-eyes me. "Eating it, and enjoying the hell out of it. I rarely eat anything other than chicken and veggies."

"Are you serious?"

"What?" he says through a mouthful of fries. "I try to eat healthy. I *am* an athlete, you know. We need to keep in shape to play the best game."

"Fair point."

I pop my last nugget into my mouth and gather up my trash as Caleb polishes off his burger.

"Thank you for that, Zoe." He shoves his wrapper into the bag and sips the last of his Powerade before shoving that inside too. "I mean, I'm definitely going to regret it later, but damn was that good."

"You're welcome...I think."

"I'm gonna run these to the trash really quick. Lock the door behind me."

I glance around, surprised he'd make that suggestion. "We're sitting in a Frankie's parking lot at eight thirty on a Tuesday. I don't think anything is going to happen in the forty seconds it'll take you to toss this out."

"Are you always so argumentative? The entire time in the store, you were the same way."

"I don't *argue*. I tactfully sway your opinions in my favor."

"So you argue until you get your way."

"Sure, if that's how you want to see it."

He lifts his eyes skyward and sighs. "Just do it."

He pushes the door open and steps out, slams it closed, and waits.

I glare at his form through the window as he stands there. He won't budge until I lock the damn door.

After what feels like several minutes, I give in and click the button.

He scurries away, and I watch him move effortlessly. His walk is determined and sure—and I feel like a damn moron for noticing, especially in this moment.

Before I know it, he's knocking on the window, I'm unlocking the door, and we're back on the road, heading to the apartment.

We're quiet, and as much as I'm enjoying the calmness, there's something weighing on my mind that I want to talk about.

His hand.

I've known who Caleb Mills was since the moment I stepped foot on campus. *Everyone* knows who he is: star third baseman for the Hawks. He's always been popular, known throughout the university as the guy who's always there, the one you can count on.

Being so easy on the eyes has brought him attention too. I think every girl on campus has crushed on him at some point in her time here, but not once has he earned a reputation as anything other than a gentleman. Until Delia, there were always jokes flying that he was the only virgin Hawk on the team. I don't think anyone actually thought that was true, but still.

No one has ever said a bad thing about Caleb, so him getting into a scuffle? I want to know what the hell happened.

"Can I ask you something?"

"Shoot."

"Your hand..."

He groans at my words, I'm sure because he knows what's coming next.

"Yeah?" The word is gruff, full of contempt—not at me though; at the situation.

"You said it happened during a fight?"

"Yep."

"With who?"

"No one important." His words are almost whispered, and I can hear the regret in them.

"You broke your hand over no one important?"

He sighs loudly and gives me a clipped nod. "Yep."

"How bad is it?"

"It's bad. I'm probably done."

I peek over at him. He's staring out the passenger window, angular scruff-covered jaw clenched tight. I can feel the heat coming off him, and I wish I hadn't broached the subject at all.

But it's too late to turn back now.

"Like...*done* done?"

"*Done* done."

I let out a breath, and he shifts in his seat like talking about it is making him physically uncomfortable.

"What about... I thought you were playing with some junior league team next year?"

The corners of his mouth quirk up. "Not junior league, babe, minor, and it was never official. We were just in talks, but now it's completely off the table."

Babe.

I don't know if it's that word or what he just confessed that knocks the breath out of me. "Wow," is all I can manage.

"Yep, wow."

Sadness seeps out of his voice and I want to reach out to him, tell him how sorry I am that he's lost his dream.

I know if anything happened to my hands and I couldn't pick up a pencil or paintbrush anymore, I'd be lost.

And that's exactly what Caleb sounds like right now.

"Did you at least win?"

A chuckle escapes his lips and he shakes his head, pulling his cap off and running a hand through his thick mess of curls. He stares down at his lap with a grin, fiddling with the cap and bending the rim to just the right position.

"Well?" I tease.

"Yeah, I won."

"Good."

I ease the SUV into a parking space and neither of us speak as we load our arms with bags of groceries and walk them up to the apartment.

"Do you have a certain way you want this arranged?" he asks once we've brought everything inside.

He begins pulling things from the paper bags and I notice the way he favors his left hand, the one not in a brace. He's been doing that the entire night—at the store, while we were eating, and now. I want to ask him more about his injury, but I also want to give him space on the subject.

"Not really. I don't use my cabinets much."

"Mind if I rearrange?"

"Have at it."

I pour a glass of the fresh-squeezed orange juice we bought and take a seat at the countertop bar. Caleb drags his phone from his pocket and clicks a few buttons.

"We have Wi-Fi, right?"

"This isn't the dark ages. Of course we have Wi-Fi."

"Password?"

"XGonGiveItToYa69. Caps the beginning of each word."

He gives me a blank stare. "Is this more of that Breakfast and Beats shit?"

"Or the fact that DMX is *amazing*."

"Sure, or that." He plugs the password in and swipes around a few different screens. "How'd you get so into rap? You don't really seem..."

"The type? Why, because I'm an artist and I should be all about that mopey emo shit?"

He shakes his head, flustered. "N-No, that's not what I was saying."

"Wasn't it?"

Grinning, he says, "Okay, maybe a little."

"Thought so."

"Seriously, how'd you get into it?"

"I'm really not *that* into it, just what's on my B&B playlist. I like how jazzed up it makes me feel, gets my blood pumping in the morning, which helps get my creativity flowing. Ninety-nine percent of the time, I listen to that mopey emo shit." I grin at him.

"Aha! I knew it!"

I shrug. "What can I say? I'm a walking artistic cliché. What about you? What kind of music do you like?" I twist my lips up as I study him. "I want to say you're a top 40s guy based off the whole *aw shucks*, boy-next-door thing you have going on, but I also kind of want to say classic rock since you've already surprised me once before."

He laughs. "I have an 'aw shucks' thing going on? What does that even mean?"

"You know." I stand and make my way to the fridge, pulling out the juice and refilling my cup. I rest against the counter, take a drink, and shrug. "Irresistible blue peepers, blond curly hair. The dimple in your chin. That body. That cute grin you hand out like candy on Halloween night. Your obliviousness to how hot you are. The fact that you're kind of a closet nerd. You know, all of that."

Caleb crosses his arms over his chest, his muscles straining against the material of his shirt, and leans against the counter. His eyes are trained on me, full of mischievous fun and something else.

He takes me in from head to toe, his stare so full of heat I can feel sweat licking at my skin. We're standing only a foot apart, something palpable hanging between us.

Pushing off the counter, he takes a step toward me and leans close. Those safe couple feet of distance that separated us only moments ago have become nothing but inches, and my heart begins beating against my chest wildly at his proximity, his scent almost overwhelming me. My Brown Sugar Pear body wash is the first thing I smell, but beyond that is a whole different scent.

All man.

All Caleb.

"You been paying attention to me, Zoe?"

Blood rushes to my ears, nearly drowning out his words. The invisible string is pulled taught and there's no air left in the room.

There's something in his words, in the calm, soft tone he uses.

He's not asking to embarrass me. He's asking to *encourage* me.

"You're hard to miss, Caleb."

His eyes darken and flit to my parted lips, remaining there for far longer than appropriate.

We stand there, inspecting one another, waiting for…I don't know what. To make a move, to bring our mouths closer, to do anything other than just stand here…

My grip is waning on the glass I'm holding, and I wonder how many seconds it'll be before it slips out of my hand completely.

Suddenly Caleb rears back and retraces his steps to the safe two-foot distance we had before, his attention turning firmly to his phone.

He's good at that—retreating, pulling himself away.

He also plays into the silent broody thing a lot more than I thought he would. He's keen on using as few words as possible to get his point across.

Part of me likes it. The other part wants to scream out in frustration.

Slowly, my heart begins to calm, my breathing returning to normal.

This isn't the first time today we've leaned into one

another, not the first time his eyes stayed trained on my lips for a beat too long or the first time I've wanted to press against him, wanted to touch him in any way I can.

There's something about Caleb that's magnetic, enticing me closer with each passing moment.

If I'm not careful, he'll reel me all the way in.

There's no turning back from that.

A soft, bluesy tone drifts through the surround sound speakers in the living room, and it pulls me back into the moment and away from the dangerous thoughts bouncing around inside my head.

I laugh at what I hear playing.

"See? I knew you'd be into classic rock. Zeppelin's a good choice."

He shrugs and starts pulling boxes of mac and cheese from the cabinets, organizing them on the counter so he can make room for the new groceries we bought. "Guess I'm a predictable guy."

"Far from it." I return to my spot at the counter. "I never expected that massive comic book collection you have."

"*That's* what surprised you?"

"You scream jock, not nerd."

He chuckles. "I suppose that's a fair point since I *do* play baseball." The can of corn he's holding is suspended in midair as he halts all movements.

His broad shoulders sag and I itch to reach out to him,

to comfort him in his obvious pain. I hate that he lost something that meant so much to him.

"*Did.* I did play baseball."

"Even still," I say immediately, moving on and hoping he does too. "You have that look about you. I don't think of you being the first to the store when the new issue hits or waiting in line at cons, but based on the number of comics you have and the stacks of badges I saw, you've done both...*a lot.*"

"No? Then what do you think?"

"Friday nights beneath the lights, keggers on the weekends, homecoming—you know, good guy homegrown boy stuff."

A huffed laugh escapes him and he shakes his head. I don't know if he's amused or annoyed. "You're way off base, Zoe."

"How so?"

He moves around the kitchen, ignoring my question as he continues to empty and then refill the cabinets just how he wants them.

Finally, when he's putting up the last pile of groceries, he responds. "I wasn't homegrown. I just was."

I sit there, blinking, unsure what exactly his words are supposed to mean. I'm stunned by the way he drops what he's doing and marches out of the room, bad attitude in tow.

He doesn't slam his door closed, but the message is loud and clear: *leave me be.*

My brows pinch together as I stay seated at the counter, chewing my bottom lip and staring at the spot Caleb was occupying only moments ago.

Did I pry too much? Was I too invasive? Are questions about his past off limits? Does it get that dark?

Not once did I get the vibe from Caleb that he was carrying around anything but sunshine. He's always been that easygoing, happy guy. I assumed he had the golden childhood, parents still together, prom king and all that.

But the light that shines off him isn't a reflection of his past, a dark gray area I never knew existed; it's a glimpse into his future, a demonstration of the person he strives to be.

MY PHONE VIBRATES against my bedside table, and I'm hesitant to put down my paintbrush for it.

I'm in the middle of what I like to call a *get this stupid shit off my mind* piece. Basically, I'm going balls to the wall and letting my hands take control.

There's another buzz.

"Ugh."

With reluctance, I put my brush down and snatch up the offending object.

This better be damn good.

Caleb: I'm sorry…sorry I walked away and didn't talk anything over with you. I suck sometimes and tonight was one of those times.

Caleb: Can you forgive me?

Well, look at the balls on him.

Me: Prepare for a lengthy response…

Me: I'm pretty pissed at you, a little confused, and maybe even hurt. For one, I didn't deserve that sort of exit. For two, you didn't even finish cleaning up the kitchen. That's not good roomie behavior. I don't know what kind of roommates you had before, but I'm not about to walk on eggshells around you and your temper tantrums. Let me in, keep me shut out—I don't give a crap. Just don't treat me that way and we'll be square. Check your shit at the door and don't take it out on me.

Caleb: Yeah. Roger that.

Me: Did you really just act like an ass again?

Caleb: Shit, I did. I'm sorry. I fucking suck.

Me: You're damn right you do.

Caleb: It's just…my past is a sore subject for me. I'm sure you've figured that out by now.

Me: No shit. That bad?

Caleb: Dick stuck in a zipper bad.

Me: I don't have a dick, as we've already established, so I don't know what that feels like, but it doesn't sound fun.

Caleb: Oh, there was nothing fun about it. I wasn't the golden child. I didn't get invited to parties, let alone a school dance. I wasn't homecoming anything. The only reason I was part of the baseball team and was able to get the fuck out of that place was because of my mom and who she was and what she did for the coaches after hours. I skated the edges of the outcasts and barely outran the troubled ones. High school was tough. College is my do-over.

Caleb: Think we could get a do-over?

Me: I can do that, but this is your last chance. Don't screw it up.

Me: God, I feel like we're all keyed up here now. Can't we just go back to flirting like we did in the emails?

Caleb: Flirting? Is that what you were doing? Oh, you mean go back to you staring at my ass and me pretending like I don't notice? Or you inching close to me and trying to get me to give in to kissing you? You want to go back to that?

Me: You are such a jerk! I was NOT staring at your ass.

Me: Okay, fine. I was. So sue me. You've got a great ass.

Me: I hate you because now I'm blushing, and I never blush. WHAT HAVE YOU DONE TO ME?

Caleb: You are such a liar. You could never hate me. Even when I'm at my worst, you won't be able to truly hate me. Don't worry, I won't tell anyone you were checking me out…if you promise not to tell anyone I was checking you out too.

Caleb: P.S. THAT'S how you flirt.

Me: Oh, everyone already knows you were checking me out because they were too. I'm hot. *shrugs*

Caleb: You are like a female version of Zach. You know that, right?

Me: Point?

I smack my hand against my forehead.

Flirting? Really, Zoe? Ugh.

As much as Caleb has annoyed me tonight, I can't help but be drawn in by him. He's so...different than I expected, so much more complex.

I want to get to know him more, and that's how I get to know people—I flirt.

It's who I am, and I've never been ashamed of that.

Flirting is harmless...*right?*

CHAPTER 6

"WHAT IN THE hell are you watching?"

I let out a loud yelp and jump, sending the bowl of cereal I'm eating flying all over me and the couch. My phone goes soaring across the room as the hand that was holding it goes to my chest.

I shoot off the couch and spin toward Caleb, milk dripping down my chin and soaking my t-shirt. "What is wrong with you? You scared the shit out of me!"

"You did not poop."

"Figuratively. I figuratively shit myself."

"And you got cereal all over you."

"Oh?" I wipe at my chin. "Did I now?"

"You did, and that shirt you're wearing? Well, let's just say it's thin."

I glare over at him. "Be a gentleman and get me a towel."

Caleb laughs his way to the kitchen and grabs the hand towel hanging from the stove. He casually saunters back my way and holds it out.

"This had better come out," I mutter, scrubbing at the mess, thankful most of it landed on my blanket.

"You can't seriously be mad at me."

"I'm irritated. Two different things."

"For walking into my living room?"

"You didn't announce yourself!"

"It's *my* living room too!"

Caleb and I have been living together for about a week and a half now and I'm *still* not used to him. Sure, a lot of that has to do with the fact that we don't spend much time together with our hectic schedules, but it's more because he's so...*quiet*. He's like a damn ninja sneaking around the apartment.

"But you need to be louder!"

"Would you like me to *stomp* through the apartment?"

"Could you please?"

"No." He grabs the towel and my soiled blanket, hauling them down the hall.

I follow him, marching into my room and stripping off my shirt. I wrench open my drawer and pull out another shirt.

"I'm sor—holy shit those are your boobs."

Caleb stands in my doorway, face turning redder and redder as the moments pass. He inhales a sharp breath but exerts no effort to move or cover his eyes.

Nothing.

We stand there in shock because I'm not wearing a shirt.

I am not wearing a fucking shirt, and I am standing in front of Caleb in just my black lace bra.

His eyes roam over my scantily clad skin, his pupils dilating as he takes me in, clearly liking what he sees—and speaking of seeing, I'm certain he notices the way my chest begins to rapidly move up and down as his gaze rakes over me in the most sensual way possible.

It's not predatory, and it doesn't make me feel gross.

It makes me feel good, empowered.

Sexy.

And it's all because of Caleb.

Shit, shit, shit! Caleb shouldn't be making me feel sexy. *This* should not be happening right now.

I grab at the shirt nearest me and hastily pull it over my head, covering myself.

I glare at him. "This! This is why you need to start announcing yourself, Caleb. I was changing!"

He lifts his hands and finally covers his eyes. "I wasn't trying to perv on you, I promise. I just didn't think. I'm not used to living with girls."

I want to berate him, to dig into him and give him a good tongue-lashing, but that feels so wrong when his eyes on my body felt so good.

"Well you better get used to it," I huff out as I storm past him and back down the hallway to the living room.

I grab my bowl and walk it into the kitchen.

"I am coming down the hallway!" Caleb yells. "I am now exiting the hallway!"

I roll my eyes and walk back into the living room, snatching up my phone on my way through.

"I am entering the living room!"

I take a seat on the couch, curling back up under the other blanket we keep there.

"I am sitting on the couch!" he hollers as he plops onto the cushions.

"You are being a pain in the ass!"

"Hey, I'm just trying to announce myself, as requested."

"I didn't mean in every situation."

He looks around the couch. "Is that the last blanket now that you've spilled milk all over the other one?"

I pull said blanket around me tighter. "Yep."

"Well shit. It's cold as hell. Why do you keep it freezing in here?"

"Because I'm hot."

He gives me a teasing grin. "I know, but that's not what I was asking about."

"I mean I *get* hot easily. I'd rather be freezing my tits off than sweating. Just deal with it."

Suddenly he reaches out and pulls the blanket off me with one quick yank.

"What in the hell!" I shout.

"What? I'm cold."

"Caleb!"

"Yes, my dear sweet roommate?"

"Give it back."

"Nope." The word pops out of his mouth in the just the perfect way, his full lips drawing my attention.

"Caleb!"

"What?"

"Come on! Don't be a dick. I'm freezing."

"Weird, me too. That's why I have the blanket."

"It's the only one out here and I had it first," I whine.

"I know, but I'm too lazy to go grab my blanket from my room."

"Me too, which is why I was using that old raggedy one you brought with you."

"Old raggedy one, huh? Then why is it I've come home not once, not twice, but *thrice* to find you asleep on the couch with this 'old raggedy' blanket wrapped around you?"

"Pure desperation." I wave my hand, not wanting to admit that it's so much more than that.

The blanket smells like him, like warmth and comfort and Caleb all wrapped in one. It's so...*cozy*, but I'm not about to tell him that.

"Uh huh," he says in a tone that tells me he doesn't believe that for a second.

He's not wrong.

"Just shut up and give me the blanket back."

"I will not, but we can share."

He scoots down on the couch toward me, grabbing my legs and pulling them over his lap. He shakes the blanket out around us, and just like that, we're almost cuddling.

What in the...

"Isn't this weird?" I can't help but say.

"Not if we don't make it that way."

"Huh."

"Yep."

I grab the remote and hit play, trying to turn my attention to the screen, trying to ignore how good it feels to be so close to Caleb, to overlook how normal and comforting it is.

It's just Caleb. You've known him for months. He's just your roommate. Don't make this weird.

Right. Don't make it weird. Don't let him know I'm totally crushing on him.

Right.

Just then my phone buzzes across the table and I reach over, scooping it up.

I'm surprised to see Delia's name flashing on the home screen. It's late and she's usually so grandma-like and thus already in bed at this hour.

> Delia: Okay, it's been long enough now, and I've been dying to ask—how's it going with Caleb?

> Me: You never told me he was so moody.

> Delia: Surprise!

> Delia: He can be quite the handful, but he's a good guy.

Me: Yeah, I don't doubt that at all. It's going to be...interesting living with him, that's for sure.

Delia: Well don't let our past interfere with anything, you know. Just treat him like you would any other roommate.

Me: I will. He's fun so far. Funny. A little flirty even. I think it's going to be good living with him.

Delia: That's Caleb for ya, endless flirt and the life of the party. I'm happy to hear that, Zoe. I was worried you were going to hate me forever for bailing on you.

Me: I could never hate you...unless you did something REALLY awful, like burned all my rap CDs.

Delia: I cannot believe you even still own CDs. You and Zach, you're both so...OLDSCHOOL.

Me: Don't hate us 'cause you ain't us.

Delia: Ya know, that's exactly what he would say.

Delia: You're both exhausting. Good night.

Me: Night. XO

Treat him like any other roommate.

She's right. I need to do that. I need to treat him like

he's just Caleb, not like he's her ex...not like we have some weird scrambled history together.

He's *just* Caleb.

Just *Caleb*.

If that's true, why does my heart beat a little faster when he's around? Why does my breathing pick up like I've just climbed fifty flights of stairs? Why is all my attention focused on him?

Every time he comes home from his late nights at work or at study sessions, I hear him, and I lie awake in my bed listening, waiting...for what? I don't know, but I feel so... tuned in to him.

Which is so stupid because we haven't spent that much time together, and when we do, it involves grocery shopping and him annoying me until I laugh.

But still...there's something there, something sitting just beneath the surface.

"What in the hell are we watching?" he finally enquires after the episode is nearly half over.

"*Parenthood.*"

"Like that old movie with Steve Martin in it?"

"No. Well...sort of. This is a very loose adaptation of it."

"It's..."

"Sad? I know. I cry like every episode."

"That is not what I was going to say at all. Wait, that chick...is that Lorelai Gilmore?"

I pause the show and stare at him. "You know who Lorelai Gilmore is?"

He lifts a shoulder. "We had TV and they showed these things called reruns. It was on one of the three stations we got."

"And *you* watched it?"

"What? She's hot."

I fall into a fit of laughter. "Total dude response."

"She's got fire, kind of like you, lots of spunk—I like that."

"Like me? You like my spunk?" I can feel my lips twitching at the words.

He narrows his eyes. "Don't be a perv, but yes, I like your *spunk.*"

"I like your spunk too, Caleb."

"Zoe! It's not as funny when you say it. It's more...*real!*"

"What? You can be all pervy but I can't?"

"I wasn't being pervy at all. That was you! You sure do like to leave your mind in the gutter."

"I can't help it," I say, tapping my temple. "It's like a twelve-year-old boy up in here."

He shakes his head. "Oh, I can tell. I can fucking tell."

I give him a gentle kick. "You like it, and me."

Caleb glances over at me with a look in eyes that's something a little more than friendly. "I do."

I rest back against the couch, not asking him to clarify what he meant because part of me doesn't want to know.

As silly as it is, I like this flirty thing we have going on. On one hand, it feels strange because he's Delia's ex, but on the other hand it doesn't, because it's just who I am. It feels natural, and if I'm supposed to be treating him like any other roommate, this is exactly what I'd be doing.

Right?

"I'll be leaving early in the morning," he says.

"Because it's Sunday?"

"Yep. I'll be back late tomorrow night...I hope."

"Do you want a ride?"

"No, I got it."

"Do you want to tell me where you're going?" I try to push.

"Not yet." His response is stoic, but that word he put there—*yet*—it implies that maybe one day he *could* tell me where he goes.

Huh.

"Are we really going to keep watching this?"

"Yes, Caleb, we're really going to keep watching this."

He lets out a loud groan and snuggles into the couch more, but I don't miss the way his eyes don't stray from the TV screen once.

He likes it, and he likes me.

I grin to myself and focus back in on the latest Braverman drama.

I WAKE up to the growling voice of Hatebreed's *Seven Enemies* reverberating off the walls.

A body shifts beneath me and I freeze.

Caleb.

Oh hell. We fell asleep together on the couch, somehow tangling ourselves up more than we were before. I'm practically draped across him. I remember moving at some point during the night, flipping around so my neck wasn't propped on the arm of the couch. I remember Caleb's voice whispering, "Shh, just sleep," in my ear as he pulled my head into his lap and ran his fingers through my hair. It lulled me back to sleep in no time.

I glance to the clock hanging near the front door, checking to see what time it is. *Two AM.* Who in the hell is calling this late at night?

"Hello?"

I don't move and barely breathe, trying not to alert Caleb to my consciousness as he answers his phone in a sleepy drawl.

"Yeah. Yeah."

He lets the person on the other end of the line speak, and I can faintly hear their voice. Whoever it is, it's a woman, and she isn't happy at all.

"I got it."

Another raised voice.

"I got it, *Mom.* I'll bring them."

Mom? Why is his mother calling at this hour?

"I said I will bring them. Have I ever not before?" He's

practically growling the words out at this point. "Yeah. *Yes.* I will. *Now?*"

He lets out a long sigh and runs a hand over his head.

"Yeah. I'll leave now."

He ends the call and throws his phone onto the other end of the couch.

"Son of a fucking bitch," he mutters. "Dammit. Mother*fucker.*"

I can feel it as he scrubs his hands over his face, hear as he scrapes over his five o'clock shadow.

He's irritated, and I can't say I blame him. It's early as shit and unless it's an emergency, there's no reason he needs to leave for his Sunday trip right now.

I want to sit up and tell him all this, but it's not my place. It's not my business.

He carefully scoots out from under me and I lie there, listening as he moves about the apartment and gathers his things.

He's quick, only taking about five minutes to get ready.

I do everything in my power not to jump when I sense him standing over me, when his fingers gingerly meet my cheek. He swiftly brushes a lock of hair back from my face and then just as fast, he's gone, grabbing his bag and disappearing out the front door.

My phone chimes not even three minutes later.

> Caleb: I'm off for my Sunday funday. I'll see you later.

I don't respond. Instead I place my phone back on the table and sit up, curling his blanket around me.

I don't fall back asleep.

I don't move until the sun comes up.

I sit there, thinking about Caleb...about the phone call, his hand, his anger toward his past...about everything involving him.

He was right to masquerade as The Riddler.

Caleb's an enigma through and through.

CHAPTER 7

Me: Okay, it has officially been three days since I've seen you. You came back from your Sunday outing, made me an omelet for breakfast, and then disappeared again. I'm starting to think I made you up.

Caleb: I told you my schedule was insane. This week is going to be hell for me. Shift after shift, study group after study group, and class after fucking class. Don't forget all the other little shit I have to do in between.

Caleb: Friday the 12th is my next day off.

Me: THAT IS NEXT FRIDAY! WHAT THE HELL!

Caleb: Tell me about it. I need a damn nap.

Me: You really don't have a day off until then?

Caleb: Fully off? No. I'll have some time to sleep and maybe a few hours in the mornings every now and then.

Caleb: How's Mittens doing, by the way? I saw your door was cracked last night and when I couldn't find him I assumed he was with you. Sorry kitten duty has fallen to you.

Me: Don't you ever apologize for allowing me to snuggle that adorable fluffball all night long.

Me: He's good. He was a little skittish at first, but we've worked it out. Now he won't leave me be. I had to repaint a spot that was drying last night.

Caleb: Shit. Sorry about that.

Caleb: My hours are officially cut starting next Thursday. I'll still be gone on Sundays, but I'll only be working one double instead of four days a week after classes. I'll be out some money, but the sleep and study time will be nice, especially with finals slowly approaching.

Caleb: Why'd you ask when I'd be home next? You missing me already, Zoe?

Me: I miss your cooking. You? Not so much.

Me: Thanks for making enough dinner for leftovers when I was at work last night. My stomach and my co-workers love you.

Caleb: I'm not too bad of a cook, huh? Learned that shit growing up in the trailer park too.

Me: I'm impressed.

Me: I'm sorry, but it is INSANE how our schedules don't line up, right? I'll be at work and you'll be at work. I'll be home and you'll be at work. You'll be home and I'll be in class. What kind of shit is that?

Me: Though I did hear you in the shower this morning. You sounded a bit…preoccupied. ;-)

Me: (THAT WAS A MASTURBATION JOKE.)

Me: Caleb, you there? I'm bored. There's a project I could be working on, but nothing is inspiring me. Nothing is speaking to me. I hate that part about being an artist sometimes—you have to wait for that spark when you just want to hit the ground running. Hard balance to maintain.

Me: I guess you're busy and I'm just rambling anyway. Good night.

Caleb: Sorry. Study group ran late last night and then I didn't want to be the rude ass passenger on the way home. Then I just passed out once I sat down on my bed, and now it's early morning so you're probably in class.

Caleb: Don't think I haven't heard your late-night moans, Zoe. The walls in our apartment are thin. (MASTURBATION TRUTH, NOT JOKE)

Caleb: I can't imagine being an artist. One, I don't have the skill. I'm a horrible drawer. Two, I don't have the imagination. Nothing speaks to me the way baseball does, but now I don't even really have that anymore.

Caleb: I won't lie, I'm bummed about my hand. I was excited as hell when the minors wanted me, even talked myself into doing it and trying for the majors, but now that'll never happen. The fracture wasn't enough that I need surgery, but I messed up a tendon and nerve. So yeah, my grip is gone. I'm screwed.

Caleb: Anyway, I guess it will all work out. Good thing I have a backup plan, and there's always coaching. Now I'm rambling. Good night.

Me: I hate that you lost baseball, especially since I know you're not a fighter. Whatever/whoever it was about must have been something special if you put your dream on the line for it.

Me: Also, the walls aren't THAT thin. Ass.

Caleb: They ARE that thin. Maybe you should pipe down, and maybe one day I'll tell you the story about my hand—if you're lucky.

Me: Dear Ghost Roomie, you get to see me this week. How excited are you?

Caleb: I'm not.

Me: LIAR!

Me: You miss me, and you know it.

Caleb: Missing you is a stretch. I haven't known you long enough as a roommate to miss you. I do miss your cookies though. ;-)

Me: Uh huh. Trying to use a euphemism there I see, but you failed—you've never had my COOKIE, now have you? Nice try, loser.

Caleb: It's the thought that counts.

Me: YOU WERE THINKING ABOUT MY VAGINA?

Me: Is THIS flirting?

Caleb: This is me running on energy drinks and naps for the last two days. Cut me some slack, yo.

Me: I heard you come in about midnight last night after your mysterious Sunday out. I was THIS close to bothering you, but I didn't want you to see what I sleep in. Now I'm glad I stayed away.

Caleb: NAKED? Do you sleep naked?!

Me: Wouldn't you like to know. ;-)

Caleb: Honestly? Hell yes.

Me: DOWNLOAD ATTACHMENT

Caleb: Not just your retainer but zit cream too? Be still, my beating heart.

Me: Right? You're welcome. Keep that one for later.

Caleb: Remember how you offered for your friend to grab my bike for me?

Me: I do.

Caleb: Well…

Me: Spit it out.

Caleb: My old roommates are threatening to have it towed, saying I'm blocking their parking. Think you could help me out?

Me: You don't come home, you don't call, yet you want favors. Hmm… decisions, decisions.

Caleb: Is that a yes? I really need it to be a yes.

Me: Please hold.

Me: Okay, Robbie can help.

Caleb: And he'll take good care of my baby…right? I can trust this guy?

Me: Do you really have a choice right now?

Caleb: No. I can't believe these guys are being such dicks about everything. They keep saying it's because I left them "high and dry", which is complete bullshit. Fucking dicks.

Me: YEAH YOU TELL THEM

Caleb: You done?

Me: Yes.

Me: Sorry they're dicks.

Caleb: It is what it is.

Me: I'll get everything taken care of with the bike, don't you worry. Go back to your "gas station duties."

Caleb: What's with the quotation marks?

Me: Well…I have this theory.

Caleb: What was it you said earlier? Spit it out.

Me: I have this theory that you're really a stripper and you're just embarrassed and don't want to tell anyone about it. That's why you work such crazy hours and come home smelling like old ladies and sadness.

Caleb: LMAO

Caleb: Are you serious?

Me: Dead.

Caleb: Holy fuck. *dies*

Caleb: Zoe, I am NOT a stripper. I work at a 24hr gas station and that's ALL I do. I promise.

Me: I'm just saying, I wouldn't be surprised if you came home covered in glitter and wearing a G-string. *shrugs*

CHAPTER 8

Me: Mittens is an asshole.

Caleb: Oh god, what did he do?

Me: Turns out I'm a sympathy puker.

Me: He puked on my floor, and then I puked on my floor trying to clean it up. Like, I still love him and all, but I also kind of hate him right now.

Caleb: Shit. He probably ate too fast. I'm so sorry you have to deal with that, Zoe. I promise I'll be at home more often and all the kitten duty won't fall to you.

Caleb: I'll make you dinner.

Me: You already cook for me. Try again.

Caleb: I'll…hmm…

Caleb: I'll touch your butt.

Me: Who's really getting the most of that one?

Caleb: That wasn't a no...

Me: We'll see. ;-)

Caleb: How about...I'll TAKE you out to dinner.

Me: Did you just ask me out on a date? I thought we talked about you trying to stick your ham in my meat wallet.

Caleb: No. Do not say meat wallet. And it's not a DATE date, just like a roomies date. Ya know, for not sucking.

Me: But...what if I like sucking?

Caleb: Did you just make a blow job joke?

Me: ...Yes.

Caleb: I...I was not expecting that.

Caleb: You never stop surprising me.

Me: Is that a bad thing?

Caleb: Not at all.

Caleb: Unless you're surprising me with herpes or something. Then that's bad.

Me: Noted.

Me: DID YOU USE MY BODY WASH AGAIN?!

Caleb: Define use…

Me: DID YOU SQUIRT IT ON YOUR LOUFA AND USE ALL MY GODDAMN BODY WASH, CALEB MILLS?!

Caleb: Define all…

Me: CALEB!

Caleb: ZOE!

Me: CALEB!!

Caleb: ZOE!!

Me: DOCTOR SCOTT!

Caleb: Uh…what? This is Caleb still.

Me: No. Noooooo. Puh-lease tell me you've seen that movie.

Caleb: What movie?

Me: THE BEST FUCKING MOVIE EVER!

Caleb: Field of Dreams?

Me: Omg. You would. You fucking would.

Me: No. Try again.

Caleb: The Sandlot?

Me: NO DAMMIT.

Me: The Rocky Horror Picture Show. OBVIOUSLY.

Caleb: The what?

Me: You've never watched Rocky Horror?

Caleb: I have not.

Me: That's it. We're doing it.

Caleb: It? Like sex? Are we having sex?

Caleb: How did this turn into us banging?

Me: No! We're going to see Rocky Horror. It's a whole experience—toast and rice and water guns and yelling. You're going to love it. We'll go this month.

Caleb: I don't know how we went from talking about movies to sex and now toast. Are you drunk?

Me: We were never talking about sex!

Me: And no, I'm not drunk. I wish.

Me: Bring me wine.

Caleb: No.

Me: You're so mean.

Me: So, are you in for Rocky Horror?

Caleb: Sure. I guess. When is this?

Me: Third Thursday of every month. Midnight.

Caleb: MIDNIGHT? Are you off your damn rocker, woman? No way. That's way past my bedtime.

Me: IT IS NOT. You don't come home until one or two in the morning half the time.

Caleb: But my hours are changing, remember? I'm implementing a new bedtime. Right after Wheel of Fortune, I'm hitting the sack, no ifs, ands, or butts about it.

Me: Are you an ass man, Caleb?

Caleb: ...No.

Caleb: Fine. Yes.

Caleb: I'm ASSuming you caught that?

Me: You've ASSumed correctly.

Me: DOWNLOAD ATTACHMENT

Caleb: Did you just really send me a picture of a donkey?

Me: What? You said you were an ass man.

Caleb: You are SUCH a smartass.

Me: Excuse me, I prefer smartdonkey.

Caleb: *rolls eyes*

Me: Rocky Horror date is set. That's where you can take me for making me clean up your kitten's puke. You owe me…

Caleb: *sighs* Fine.

Caleb: I gotta go back to work now. Smoke break's over.

Me: You smoke?

Caleb: Gross. No. But they don't know that. ;-)

Me: You're incorrigible.

Caleb: You're not erroneous.

Me: I see what you did there…though I don't think that's the right context.

Caleb: It's the thought that counts.

Me: Okay, okay. I'm sorry I yelled at you yesterday. Thank you.

Caleb: I see you got my gift. You're welcome.

Caleb: Also, do you have any idea how expensive 6 bottles of that body wash is? Roughly six billion dollars.

Me: Wait a second here…6 bottles? I only see 3.

Me: Holy crap. Did you go for the buy 3 get 3 free deal and KEEP THEM?

Caleb: Maybe…

Me: So yes.

Caleb: Hey, you can't blame me! That stuff smells amazing. I mean, even I'd lick me right now.

Me: I would too.

Caleb: You'd lick me too?

Me: NO.

Me: But also maybe yes.

Me: Wait…nah.

Caleb: I'm going with yes as your final answer.

Me: Aren't you supposed to be working?

Caleb: I'm at study group.

Me: Oh shit. Then why are you texting me? Go learn something.

Caleb: Because you texted me first, and then you started talking and just wouldn't stop.

Me: Are you trying to tell me I never shut up?

Caleb: In the nicest way possible.

Me: You're so good to me, Ghost Roomie.

Caleb: I'm not a ghost for much longer.
Just two more damn days and then I'm
free.

Caleb: Convince me not to rage-quit.

Me: Hmmm...I'm not sure I can do that
without specifics here.

Caleb: I put in to have the night off when
that horror movie you want to take me
to is playing, but they fucking scheduled
me anyway. Assholes.

Me: I'm not going to lie, I'm laughing so
hard right now.

Caleb: This is a time of crisis. This is
NOT the time to laugh.

Me: Rocky Horror is NOT a horror
movie. It's a musical.

Caleb: I'm sorry...you want ME to watch
a musical?

Caleb: You just talked me off my rage-
quit cliff. Thanks, pal.

Me: NO! We. Are. Going. Offer up that sexy body of yours to your co-workers to get them to switch shifts with you or something.

Caleb: Two things. ONE: Did you just ask me to exchange sex for a night off to watch a musical? TWO: Did you just call me sexy? *waggles brows*

Me: ONE: Yes. TWO: Don't pretend you don't know you're dead sexy.

Caleb: DEAD sexy, huh? That's like, sexy times 10.

Caleb: You so want me.

Me: I want you to bang your co-worker so we can go see Rocky Horror, yes.

Caleb: Yeah, not happening. I'll figure it out.

Me: So that means you WANT to go see the show?

Caleb: No, it means I made a promise and a deal is a deal.

Caleb: Plus, I'm hoping you're going to let me touch your butt at some point.

Me: Stop flirting and go work.

Caleb: So bossy. Me likey. ;-)

Me: *groans*

I WAS WRONG.

There's a whole lot of wrong flirting can do.

It can make you miss someone, make you crave them, make you *want* them more than you already do, especially when you're not supposed to want them at all.

I hate flirting, but I can't stop it now.

Just like I can't stop myself from reaching for my phone to do the same thing I've done over and over again.

Text *him*.

Me: Are you awake yet?

Caleb: Am I out there sitting next to you while you eat cereal (SHAME) and watch Rugrats?

Caleb: What channel did you find that on?

Me: No you're not, but you're obviously up, and I have it on DVD. It's called Amazon.

Caleb: Wow. Never heard of that before. /sarcasm

> Me: You're sassy first thing in the afternoon. Bum.

> Caleb: Some of us work for a living, smartass.

> Me: GASP! I work! Like ten hours a week, but still.

> Me: Just get out here or I'm coming in there.

> Caleb: No. I'm comfy.

I toss my phone onto the couch beside me and set my empty bowl of cereal on the table before pushing myself up and making my way down the hall.

"Go away," he moans as soon as I burst through the door, almost as if he was expecting me.

I pause to admire the sliver of skin that's exposed, but only for a moment. His sheet is wrapped around his lower half, shirt pushed up to display his magnificent abs. *Goddamn those abs.*

"Stop checking me out and go away."

I peel my eyes away from his body to see that he's staring at me, a smirk gracing his plump lips.

"Told ya you want me." His speech is slow and relaxed. His blond hair is a mess, his eyes tired from lack of rest.

"You wish I wanted you," I tell him as I make my way

closer to his makeshift bed on the floor and sit down next to him, my back against the wall. I leave just enough room between us so we aren't touching. I'm careful to avoid his brace, because the last thing I want to do is accidentally bump into his already fractured hand. "We really need to get you a bed. This floor has got to be killing your back."

"I don't need a bed." He closes his eyes and shimmies around until he's comfortable. "Unnecessary expense."

"Your cat has three beds. Explain that."

He lifts a shoulder. "Mittens has a bed-hoarding problem. He's in therapy for it. Don't judge him."

"We're getting you a damn bed, Caleb. We'll go shopping this weekend."

"You gonna shit out the cash to pay for one?"

"If I need to, then yes. It's not good for you to sleep on the floor. For someone who's all about keeping his body in shape, you should be aware of that."

He peeks up at me. "Fair point. I'll try to pencil you in this weekend then."

"Good. That's all I wanted."

"Is that why you came in to bother me? My lack of a bed?"

"No." I shrug. "Maybe. I'm bored."

"*Rugrats* not holding your attention?"

"It is." *But you're holding it more.* "How'd you know that's what I was watching anyway?"

"I can hear it. You're very loud, ya know."

"Sorry, I was trying to be quiet."

"You suck at it." I push at his shoulder. "What? Your footsteps sound like there's a giant clamoring around the apartment."

"They do not!"

"If you didn't have such big feet..."

I gasp. "I *do not* have big feet!"

"Whatever you say, Ronald."

"Hey!"

I shove at his arm again, and this time he reacts. I don't have the chance to make a run for it before I'm pinned halfway beneath him. He's canted off to his left side, avoiding putting much pressure on his right hand. His big hands gently hold mine captive beside my head as he smiles down at me. I don't know if I should swoon over his upper body strength or throw my panties at him.

I've always been touchy-feely with my friends, so I don't bat an eye at Caleb capturing me beneath him.

"Quit hitting me."

"I didn't hit you, I shoved you—big difference."

He closes his eyes and shakes his head. "It's too early for you to be such a donkey."

"We already talked about this—it's not early, you're just lazy."

"You're mean."

"You like it."

Caleb grins. "Maybe a little bit."

"A lot?"

"A little."

"Whatever helps you sleep at night, Caleb."

He leans into me, somehow still holding his lower half off me, and brings his lips to my ear.

That right there—the brush of his lips against my ear—that's what registers with me.

Holy fuck. Caleb's on top of me.

My heart accelerates. The thoughts running through my head are *not* thoughts I should be having, but I can't stop them from playing on repeat.

Stop it, Zoe. He's your friend, your roommate—that's it.

But I flirt with him...

I flirt with everyone!

But Caleb's different...

Fuck.

He is. He's *so* different.

Part of me feels guilty for flirting with Delia's ex-boyfriend, but they're exes for a reason, and that has to count for something...right?

"Why are you in here, Zoe?"

"I already told you—I'm bored."

His eyes find mine again. "Bored? Or you missed me?"

We stare at one another, both waiting for me to answer.

Caleb's eyes dart to my mouth and linger there. Several seconds pass before he brings his gaze back to mine.

"Well?"

I don't answer him because we both know I don't need to.

I push at him as best I can and he takes the hint, moving away in an instant. He rolls until we're lying side by side, his head resting on his pillow again.

His eyes drift closed and we surrender to the silence, lying there for several heartbeats before either of us speaks again.

"How'd you know I was eating cereal too?"

He lets out a soft chuckle. "Because I know you. I see your cereal bowls in the sink every morning. I think you're addicted to the stuff."

"Am not."

"You're a terrible liar."

I roll over until I'm facing him and watch as his chest rises and falls in a rhythmic pattern. "You're not wrong there. I couldn't even lie to my parents as a kid. I tried sneaking out once, made it all the way to the end of the driveway before the guilt ate away at me and I turned back and rang the doorbell, crying and apologizing like a moron."

"What'd they do?"

"Laughed. They had heard me climbing out my window and then watched from behind the curtains."

"See? I told you your feet were big."

I kick at him and he somehow manages to trap my feet between his legs. Neither of us makes a move to separate.

"They sound cool—your parents, I mean," he says.

"I feel like I won the lottery when it comes to them. It was touch and go for a while, but they finally found me and I got my forever family."

He turns my way, pushing himself up until he's resting his head on his hand, our feet still tangled together. "Back it up—you're adopted?"

"Delia never told you?"

"No. We didn't really talk about you though. No offense, we just didn't dig that deep into our lives."

"Does she know where you go on Sundays?" I don't know why I ask it and I don't know why I care, but I do.

"Nope."

"Good."

His eyes spark with interest at my answer, but he doesn't say anything about it. "You said it took you a while to find your family?"

"I was placed with them when I was six. They were the first ones to stick. My birth mother gave me up when I was two and then I sort of bounced around in the system. Everyone wants babies, not toddlers."

"You were two?"

"Yep."

"Can I ask...why? Do you know her?"

I shrug. "I'm not sure why, but I'm glad she did. I got Sofia and Rafe out of it, and no, I don't know her. I don't have any desire *to* know her. My parents are the only ones I need, you know?"

When you tell people you're adopted, you usually

get one of two reactions: they look at you like you're a lonely, lost puppy, or they think you're some sort of pariah.

Caleb's looking at me with something entirely different in his eyes.

Wonder. Amazement. Surprise.

"I can't imagine anyone not wanting you."

"Does that include you?" I tease.

"That includes me." He pauses and screws his face up, thinking. "Wait, no. Not me." Another pause. "What the hell...yeah, totally includes me."

"Caleb Mills, do you *want* me?"

"Define want."

"Do you want to bang me? Because I thought we talked about the no-banging rule already."

He looks at me and grins; it's wolfish. "I'll make an exception if you will."

I swallow down the *yes* I want to shout from the rooftops because I know he's only joking right now, and then I roll my eyes and playfully push his grinning face away. "Keep dreamin', bucko."

He falls onto his back, laughing and dragging me with him until my head rests on his shoulder.

"Have you been sleeping on the floor this whole time?"

"Yep."

"But it's so uncomfortable."

"What did you think I was sleeping on?" he asks.

"Honestly I figured you'd be in here snooping around with me gone all the time."

"To do what? Read your oh-so-enticing comic books?"

"Are you hating on my epic collection?"

"Never." He huffs out a sound that tells me he doesn't believe me. "Okay, maybe a little. I figured you had an air mattress or something."

"Nope. Just me, my blankets, and my pillow."

"Why don't you come sleep with me? I'm not going to be able to sleep knowing you're on the floor in here. You're an ass for not telling me you were."

"I am *not* sleeping in your bed with you." He's quick on the decision, and I have to wonder why.

"Because you're afraid you won't be able to keep your hands to yourself?"

"Yes."

I lift myself up until I can see into his eyes. "Are you serious?"

He peers back at me with a serious stare, unblinking. "Yes."

I simply nod and return to my previous position, head resting on his shoulder, our lower halves wrapped together.

We don't talk. We don't move. We don't overthink the position we're in.

We lie there, together.

Because deep down, we both know there's no denying the attraction between us.

And there's no denying we can't do anything about it.

CHAPTER 9

"RIDDLE ME THIS, roomie: it's the first Friday night we've both had off since you moved in and you're sitting on the couch...why?"

He glances away from the TV and up at me. "That's not a riddle."

"No, it's not, but it *is* a fair question."

Caleb grins, shaking his head and slouching farther into the couch. I curl my legs underneath me and take a seat, staring at him.

Moments tick by and I don't move. Neither does he.

"Are you going to do that for much longer?"

"Do what?" I ask innocently.

"Creep on me."

"Excuse me, I do not *creep*. I...admire until I'm noticed."

"So you creep."

"Sure. We'll go with that."

He aims the remote at the TV and presses pause on the episode he's watching. He makes a show of setting the clicker on the table before settling back into the couch, turning my way.

Huffing out a sigh, he says, "What do you want, Zoe?"

I twirl a lock of hair around my finger, doing my best to appear nonchalant and harmless. "Well, it's Friday."

"Yes. It's been Friday all day and it'll be Friday for several more hours. Next point."

"It's Friday and we're sitting on the couch watching Netflix."

He motions toward me, signaling for me to wrap this up. "I think we've established this too."

"Right. So, we're in agreement then?"

"Agreement about what?"

"Going out, duh."

His eyes fall to slits. "No one said anything about going out."

"I implied it."

"You did?"

"Yep. You're just a little slow at keeping up."

He nods, tucking his lips in. "Right. Sure. My bad." His voice is dripping with sarcasm. "Well go out if you want to go out."

"Together. I want to go out together. There's nothing fun about going out alone unless you're not planning to come home until the next morning."

He scratches at the two-day-old scruff on his face, contemplating that offer. "You want *me* to go out with you?" I nod. "Where? Like to a club? Dancing? Because I don't dance, period. There isn't a single rhythmic bone in my body."

"Nah. I'm not in the mood to club dance. A bar? Maybe Lola's? Something low-key."

He focuses his gaze my way. "There's a dance floor at Lola's…"

I roll my eyes. "I promise not to ask you to dance, Caleb."

Tapping his chin, he hums, thinking. "Fine. I'll go, but we need to be back by eleven, and there's a max of two beers for me. I have to be up early tomorrow and don't want to be dragging more than I already am."

"But tomorrow's Saturday."

"Wow, you really know your days of the week. Your kindergarten teacher should be proud."

"I'm sure she is, but for real, why the early wakeup?"

"I have a game."

"But…" I pause, confused. "You know the season is over, right?"

He slaps his hands over his cheeks, dropping his mouth open in faux shock. "Is it really? I had *no* idea."

"You're a real smartass tonight."

"I'm a real smartass *every* night."

"You know, I haven't really noticed that."

He coughs out a laugh. "Whoa, was that *you* being a smartass?"

"Whatever." I stand and motion for him to get moving. "Let's get going before it gets too late."

"Is that a thing? Is it ever too late for the bar?"

"Are you serious?" He nods. "You don't go out much, do you?"

"Not really."

I give my head a small shake and exhale audibly. "Wow."

"What?"

"I'm surprised is all."

"And why is that? Because I'm a baseball player?"

"Welllll...honestly? Yeah, that's exactly why."

He holds his hand to his chest, his mouth dropping open. "Are you...are you *stereotyping* me, Zoe? Do you think I catch a few balls and then head out to drink and chase girls in my free time?"

"I mean, is that *not* what you do?"

"I thought we talked about this. I wasn't that guy in high school, and that is one trait that carried over into college. Delia's only the second girl I've dated in the entire four years I've been here."

"No way."

"Yes way."

"Like *dated* dated?"

He tilts his head to the side. "Is there another kind?"

"Well, I mean...you know...like, 'dated'?"

Caleb stands to his full height, towering at least five inches above me—and I'm not short by any means. I tilt my head back to meet his eyes as he studies me, a devilish smirk on his face.

"I'm going to assume the air quotes are an indication

that you don't mean dated. You mean slept with. You asking about my sex life, Zoe? That where we're going?"

"I suppose you could say that," I say, standing my ground and stepping into him, into his warmth.

We're nearly touching, and there's no denying the electricity passing between us in this moment.

His grin grows and he leans down, his lips hovering only inches away from my ear. "I know my way around a woman's body, Zoe." My knees shake, ready to give out at any second with the way his voice lowers. "That's not something you need to be worried about."

I want to push him away and draw him closer with every word that leaves his lips...those stupid, full, kissable lips.

His eyes bore into me once more, heat blazing inside them with an unspoken promise, and just like before, I'm squeezing my thighs tight together, trying not to let his words affect me.

He brushes past me, his hard muscles sliding against my body, sending tingles to the tips of my toes.

I'm standing there alone, nearly panting over two measly little sentences like a weak, lust-driven moron.

Fucking Caleb.

"TWO LIGHT BEERS, PLEASE."

The bartender nods and scurries off to grab the drinks.

I brace my elbows on the bar top and glance out into the sea of bodies. Even for a Friday night, Lola's is extra packed. The makeshift dance floor is full of grinding bodies, every table at capacity.

I find Caleb sitting alone at a table off to the side of the bar, shoulders slumped inward as he sits there scanning the room, eyes steady and sure.

He put on a pair of jeans that cling to his legs just right and a navy blue jersey-style shirt. The first button is undone, giving the sexiest glimpse of the base of his throat. His stubble is now shaven down to a five o'clock shadow, and damn does that look suit him.

The ever-present baseball cap is sitting atop his head, this time facing the right way. I want to march over to him and spin it around. There's no reason eyes like his should be hidden in shadow.

There are a couple girls crowding the table, wanting his attention. He's not paying them any as his gaze meanders over my way, stopping only a moment to connect with my own.

I can see his lips pull up on one side then he's moving on, canvassing the room once again.

"You come here often?"

"You actually think that line will work?" I don't even bother to look at the random guy who just used the worst pickup line in the history of pickup lines.

"A guy's gotta try."

I huff out a laugh. "And that's the best you can come up with?"

I glance his way. The first thing I notice is the lack of a baseball cap, and I hate myself for even thinking about that right now because the guy standing in front of me is actually cute. His dark hair is disheveled in an artful way, grin plastered across his tan face, perfect white teeth shining out at me. He screams frat boy.

I don't do frat boys.

"Hi," he says.

"Hi."

"So, really, do you come here often? I haven't seen you before."

"Does that mean *you* come here often?"

He has the gall to look sheepish, like I don't know he's a shark in the water. "Sure, you could say that."

"Right." I turn my attention back to the bartender, brushing the guy off.

He doesn't take the hint.

"What's your name?"

I tsk. "That isn't information I hand out to just anyone."

"Oh, darlin', I'm not just anyone."

I throw my head back in laughter. "You *have* to stop with the cheesy lines. They're not getting you anywhere right now."

He stands a little straighter, his grin transforming into

something more genuine. It instantly makes him more attractive.

Sticking his hand out, he says, "Hi, I'm Tony. Care to join me for a drink?"

My eyes bounce between his hand and his face. When he's not acting like he's on the prowl, he seems like a decent guy, so I clasp his hand in mine. "Hi, Tony. Name's Zoe."

"Zoe—beautiful name for a beautiful girl."

I shake my head at him, trying to fight off a grin.

He runs a hand through his already messy hair, his embarrassment sincere. "Shit, I did it again, huh? I'm sorry. I'm horrible at this."

"First time?"

"Kind of. I just got out of a bad relationship and I'm trying to dive back into the dating game. This shit is hard, man, hence me resorting to the worst pickup lines imaginable."

"If it makes you feel any better, you're not so bad when you're not trying so hard."

"Not so bad, huh." He shakes his head, his smile broadening. "I'm such an ass because there's another line right there on the tip of my tongue and I want to say it, but I can't bring myself to do so."

I laugh. "Probably for the best."

"I'm sorry I came off as a dick. That's not who I am."

"That's exactly what a dick would say."

His eyes spark with interest. "You're a tough cookie to crack, say just what's on your mind. I like it."

"I like it too." I throw him a wink.

"Did you get lost in Narnia or something? What in the hell is taking so long?"

Caleb's warmth slams into me, that now familiar scent of his wrapping around me like a blanket. His heavy hand lands on the bar just behind me, so close that I can feel his arm resting against my back. The heat seeps through my shirt, and I can already feel the beads of sweat starting to form along the back of my neck.

"It's busy," I tell him, spinning on my stool to face him.

"Busy my ass. You were grabbing two beers. It doesn't take *that* long to pop a couple tops off."

I reach up and poke at his drawn-together brows. "You're so grumpy tonight. We're supposed to be having *fun*."

"Sitting in a room full of strangers and watching them try to score with one another is not fun. It's sad."

There's a choked cough from behind me and I realize I forgot all about my new friend Tony—who happens to be doing just what Caleb described.

"Right." I change positions on my stool until I'm facing the bar, the boys on either side of me. Caleb's free hand makes its way to my lower back, the other still attached to the bar, encasing me. "Tony, this is Caleb. Caleb, Tony. Be nice."

"I'm always nice." He pushes himself off the bar and extends his hand Tony's way. "Nice to meet you."

"Likewise." Tony catches my eye. "I'm sorry, I didn't know you were here with someone."

"Oh, I'm not. We're not together."

"Yes we are," Caleb interjects.

"What? No we aren't," I tell him.

"Yes we are."

"Are you insane? We *are not* together."

Just then the bartender slides my two beers across the counter. "Want me to start a tab, sweetheart?"

"No, but thank you." I hand over enough to cover the drinks and a tip. "You're buying the next round," I tell Caleb.

I turn back to Tony, who's staring at me with big eyes. I raise a brow at him in question.

"Nothing," he says, shaking his head. "It's nothing. I'm, uh, I'm going to go meet up with my friends. It was great meeting you, Zoe. I'm sorry to have interrupted your date."

"Date? No. That is not what this is!" But he's already retreating.

I feel the rumbling of his chest before I hear his laughter, and I nearly growl in frustration.

"You just cockblocked me!"

"I did no such thing, Zoe."

"Caleb Mills, you cockblocked me so hard I may as well be

wearing a sign on my forehead that says, 'Hey, we're together! Stay away!' Even though we most certainly are *not* together. Therefore, you should *not* be cockblocking me. Dick."

He laughs again and takes the seat Tony was just occupying. I miss the feel of his hand on my lower back the moment his fingers drift away from my skin.

"Were you really considering going home with that dude?"

"If you hadn't cockblocked me, I would have." He gives me a look of disbelief. "What? I would have gone home with him. He's my type, so why not?"

He scratches at the scruff covering his jawline. "I didn't think you were into frat boys."

I scoff, tossing my hair back over my shoulder. "Pfft. Frat boys are totally my thing."

"I don't believe you for one minute, Zoe."

"Oh, really? Well then tell me, oh wise one, what *is* my type?"

"Based on what I know about your past relationships, I'd wager to bet that your type is"—he waves a hand down his body—"well, me."

"You? You think *you're* my type? Please."

One side of his mouth lifts. "Yep. Me."

"You cannot be serious right now."

"Oh, baby, I know I'm your type."

"Just because I dated one baseball player..." Caleb lifts a brow. "Fine, just because I dated a couple baseball players does not mean I have a thing for them." His brows shoot higher and I push at his arm. "It doesn't!"

He chuckles at my feeble attempt to shove him. "Are you trying to bullshit me or yourself right now? Because we both know I'm right."

"You are not right. I'm not attracted to you."

"Right." He takes a sip of his beer, that stupid smirk still on his face.

"Fine. What if I am?"

"Then we're on an even playing field here."

"We're flirting again, right?"

"We're flirting again."

"But that's all it is, yes?"

He rolls the bottom edge of his beer bottle along the table, eyes trained on me. "If that's what you want."

"Is that what *you* want?"

"I want whatever's going to make you happiest, Zoe."

You. "Right."

It's all I say—all I *allow* myself to say.

Tonight's not about Caleb and me and our unspoken rule of allowing ourselves to toe the line but not cross it. It's about getting out of the house and having some fun.

And that's exactly what I intend to do.

I bring my beer to my mouth and take a small sip, glancing down to the other end of the bar and beyond. My eyes fall to the dance floor and I can feel that familiar ache. I'm itching to get out there. I've always loved going to the clubs and losing myself in the music, but as I've mellowed out over the years, I've resigned myself to the tiny dance floor of Lola's. Just like so many other nights, it's going to have to do for the night.

"I'm going to dance," I announce. "Watch this for me."

I set my drink on the bar top, not waiting for Caleb to respond, and head out into the crowd.

I've barely stepped into the sea of bodies and I can already feel the sweat forming along my neck and back. My body caves to the rhythm and I fall in step with the beat, losing myself to the sounds thrumming through the speakers.

"Where's your boyfriend?"

I spin around at the familiar voice to find Tony standing at the edge of the dance floor nearest me, and I make my way over to him.

Shrugging, I say, "He's not much into dancing, and he's also not my boyfriend."

He motions his head over to the bar. "Does he know that?"

My eyes follow his movements and I'm surprised to find Caleb facing the crowd, a grumpy frown lining his lips.

"Huh."

"Huh," Tony mimics.

"I swear we're not dating. He's my best friend's ex-boyfriend and my roommate."

"Take it from me, he wishes you were dating."

"You think?" I ask, eyes still trained on Caleb.

"Oh, I know."

"But he's my best friend's ex-boyfriend."

Tony laughs. "Quite the hang-up, huh?"

"For me it is."

"Girl code?" I glance his way, surprised. He shrugs. "I have sisters."

"Definitely girl code."

"You guys will figure it out."

"How are you so sure?"

"Because these things always go one of two ways: they implode, or they explode into something amazing."

"You're so encouraging. Your ex doesn't know what she's missing."

He gives me a sad grin. "Tell me about it."

"Sorry I can't date you, Tony. You seem like you'd be a great guy."

"Oh, I know I am." He winks. "I'm going to go ahead and give you my number just in case things implode." He slides a torn receipt with his name and number my way. "Use it, trash it, whatever—just can't let the opportunity pass me by."

I grin and accept it, slipping it into my back pocket. "Thank you."

I give him a small wave and dance my way back into the throng of people.

It's not long before a set of hands lands on my hips. I don't have to turn around to know it's Caleb; I know his warmth, his scent.

"I thought you didn't dance," I say to him over my shoulder, not halting my movements.

He drags me back until I'm resting against him. "I don't."

"Then what's this?"

"Swaying."

A slow song spills through the speakers just as I spin around, throwing my arms around his neck. "I'll sway with you then."

We slowly move back and forth, somehow closing the gap between us with every step we take and never once meeting the other's eyes. Our bodies are pressed together, and I'm hotter now than when the floor was overflowing.

"Hey, uh, Caleb?"

"Yep?"

"Is that your dick poking me or your phone?"

He presses his lips together, trying his hardest to hold in his laughter. "That would be my dick, Zoe."

"Oh."

Someone slams into me and I stumble, falling even farther into Caleb's embrace. He wraps his strong arms around me almost instinctively. I don't move to push away; this is exactly where I want to be right now.

The way his body feels against mine...I can't remember the last time something felt so good as we gently sway back and forth, even when the song changes.

Everyone moves so fast around us, but we don't budge. We're stuck, and we're not ready to let go of this moment.

My hands move of their own accord, tracing up his neck and sliding into the hair sticking out of his baseball cap. Without thought, I reach up and spin it around, meeting his eyes for the first time since he came out here.

"Much better." I slide my hand back down the side of his face, fingertips grazing over the stubble he's sporting.

His blue eyes darken, and before I can understand what's happening, he hauls me closer and presses his lips against mine.

It takes me a split second to realize what we're doing, and then suddenly I'm kissing him back feverishly.

Caleb manages to get ahold of himself, and then his full lips move over mine in a gentle, unhurried kiss. I feel his hands slide over my ass, his brace a firm pressure against me, pulling me closer as I plunge my hands into his hair, pulling at the ends and holding his head to mine.

There's no tongue involved, and by all accounts, the kiss is chaste, but it feels like so much more.

More romantic, more important.

Just...more.

It's minutes later when he pulls his mouth from mine, lips brushing against me twice before creating any sort of distance between us.

My lungs feel like they're on fire, mouth tingling from the best kiss I've ever experienced. I was right about our attraction to one another; I just never thought it would feel *that* good, that *right*.

When I finally come back down from the high, I open my eyes to see Caleb grinning at me.

"You got a thing for my hat, huh?"

"You've noticed in the two whole days we've spent together?"

"I noticed before."

He doesn't have to clarify that before means when he was with Delia.

And now my chest is burning for an entirely different reason.

I just kissed my *best friend's* ex-boyfriend.

I just *kissed* my best friend's *ex*-boyfriend.

I am the worst best friend ever.

He leans down to catch my drifting gaze. "You okay?"

"Yep."

"Zoe."

I arch my chin up, meeting his stare head on. "Caleb."

"Are you okay?"

I feel the sting of tears in my eyes, but I blink them away.

"I'd like to go now."

"Are you mad at me?"

"No, Caleb. I'm not mad at you."

"Then what?"

I step out of his arms and miss his heat the moment I do. It suddenly feels like I'm standing in the middle of the Arctic and not a dance floor swarming with bodies.

"Can we not? Can we do this later?"

He doesn't push the issue. He simply nods, grabs my hand, and leads me quietly from the bar.

What have we done?

IT'S one AM and I'm standing in front of Caleb's bedroom door with my pillow and blanket.

I know he's awake. There's no way he's able to sleep after the way we left things.

Slowly, I push open his door and slip inside, careful not to make a sound. I tiptoe my way to his makeshift bed and gently lay my pillow beside his resting form.

I stand over him, hesitating only a moment before finally settling myself next to him.

"I was wondering if you were going to come or not."

I adjust myself on the pillow, scooting just an inch or so closer to him. "I'm here."

Caleb lifts his arm and I slide into his embrace. Rolling over onto my side, I place a small kiss on his chest.

"I'm not sorry about kissing you."

"Me either," I whisper.

CHAPTER 10

Me: So…last night.

Caleb: Last night.

Caleb: Are you regretting it today?

Me: No. You?

Caleb: No.

Caleb: But can I tell you something?

Me: Shoot.

Caleb: I briefly regretted it, but only because I thought you'd never talk to me again.

Me: I was never mad at you, Caleb. I was mad at me.

Caleb: Why? We didn't do anything wrong, Zoe.

Caleb: You know that, right?

Me: Sure.

Me: You were gone this morning.

Caleb: I was. Little league.

Me: I bet you look so damn cute out there.

Caleb: I do.

Me: Are you wearing a ball cap right now?

Caleb: Always.

Me: *whispers* Is it backward?

Caleb: It is.

Me: I think I need to change my panties.

Caleb: I will NOT flirt with you while I'm at practice.

Me: And how many times did you have to repeat that to yourself?

Caleb: Enough.

Me: Wait, how'd you get there?

Caleb: I took the bus.

Me: CALEB! You could have asked me to give you a ride. Is that what you've been doing since you moved in?

Caleb: Mostly. Sometimes I'll catch a ride with a friend.

Me: WHY DIDN'T YOU TELL ME THIS? I would have given you rides!

Me: Seriously, I cannot believe you right now.

Caleb: I didn't want to be a bother. It's not a big deal.

Me: Is practice over yet?

Caleb: No, we still have about fifteen minutes.

Me: Are you at Cattleman's Field?

Caleb: Yes...

Caleb: Zoe?

Caleb: Hello? Zoe? What are you doing?

CALEB MILLS IS HOT.

Caleb Mills in a baseball cap? Hotter.

Caleb Mills *coaching* baseball? *Holy shit, hold my panties.*

Sitting in my car like a creeper, I watch as he stands before the team, hands on his hips and grin across his face. There's no denying that he loves the game, no disputing his complete commitment to it.

Watching him in his element is magical.

I pop open the door and casually make my way over to the bleachers, grabbing a seat closer to the action. Caleb's still giving the team a talk, and they're listening with rapt attention.

I get it, kids. I get it.

"...and I'll see you all on Wednesday. Have a good weekend."

A little girl runs up to Caleb. "Mr. C! Mr. C!" She jumps around excitedly.

He goes down on his haunches. "What's up?"

Their conversation is just out of earshot, but I love the way her face lights up when he agrees to whatever she's asked.

He helps the kids gather their things and shakes hands with a few parents before making his way over to the bleachers and taking a seat next to me.

"You didn't have to come out here, you know. I could have taken the bus."

"And miss seeing you in action?" I bump his shoulder with mine. "No way."

"Well you missed me almost getting whacked in the face by a flying bat because I was texting you."

"Shut up!"

"So serious. It came *this* close"—he pinches his fingers together—"to hitting me right in the dome."

"Little league sounds dangerous."

"I see your lips twitching."

My smile breaks through. "Sorry."

"Not sorry, right?"

"Guilty."

I rest my arms on my knees and glance out at the empty field. It looks damn near brand new, and I know that's all thanks to his college team.

"The field looks great. Your fundraiser last year must have raised a ton of money for this."

"Hell yeah it did. We brought in over $200k. Totally worth having to go on a date with that handsy seventy-year-old broad."

"Handsy, huh?"

"If it wasn't for charity, I'd have pushed myself out of that limo while it was barreling down the highway. My ass has never been touched so many times in one night before."

I laugh at the look of horror on his face. "Oh, come on, admit that you liked it just a little bit."

He shakes his head at me. "I'm not dignifying that with a response."

I bump his shoulder again. "I'm just giving you shit. Well, kind of—I do think you liked it."

"I liked it about as much as I like you right now."

"See!" I point his way. "You *did* like it."

He puffs out an irritated sigh. "You just never stop, huh?"

"That would be boring."

I glance back out at the field, smiling. He's not irritated with me, not at all. He loves the banter and endless amusement I provide—I can tell by the way his body moves closer to mine, by the constant tilt to his lips.

"You play any sports when you were younger? Or have you always been attached to that paintbrush and easel?"

"I use more than a paintbrush, but yes, I've always been attached to my art. I've never even so much as played catch before."

He spins my way, mouth dropped open in shock. "You're kidding?"

"I'm not."

Grabbing the glove he'd dropped on the bench beside him, he stands and extends his hand my way. "Let's go. We're playing catch. You have to play catch at least once in your life or you haven't lived a full life. Trust me on this."

I slip my hand into his and follow him over to his overflowing equipment bag.

"Pick a glove," he tells me.

"Any glove?"

"Yep. Just put it on and see if it fits. Make sure it feels right."

"How will I know if it feels right?"

"You'll just know."

I go through three gloves before I find one that feels comfortable.

"Good?" he asks.

"Yep. Good."

"Okay, now step out about 15 yards. We'll start there."

"Uh...yards?"

He chuckles. "Just keep walking until I tell you to stop."

I walk a few feet and glance back at him. "Here?"

"Keep going...there's good. Now, do me a favor and don't judge me for my bad throwing, okay? I don't even think I should really be doing this yet."

"We don't have to, Caleb."

Even with the distance, I can see him glower at me. "No, we're doing it. I'll just ice my hand later."

"Are you sure?"

"Yep. Now toss me the ball."

I follow the instructions he gives me then we're off to the races. I'm playing catch—rather badly I might add—for the first time in my entire life. It's kind of cool.

"How is it you've never played catch before?"

"I think it's a combination of two things: I'm a girl, and I spent some of my prime catch-playing years bouncing from home to home." I just barely catch the ball Caleb throws my way before lobbing it back at him. I cringe when he has to head far right to catch it before it hits the ground...again. "By the time I settled in with Sofia and Rafe, I was too invested in my art to pursue sports. They never pushed it either because they aren't sports people themselves, or at least they used to not be. Now they play a lot of golf."

"I guess those are valid reasons. What were you like in high school? What did you do for fun if you didn't play sports?"

"Boys."

This time he misses my first near-perfect throw out of shock.

"Zoe."

"What?" I shrug. "It's true. I had a new boyfriend every couple months my first two years."

"Just the first two years?"

Even though so much time has passed, I still feel the tiniest of tugs at my heart thinking about my high school boyfriend.

"Yep. I had a steady boyfriend the last two years."

"You guys split because of college?"

"More like split because he couldn't keep his dick to himself. He ended up getting my ex-best friend pregnant the end of senior year. Last I heard they got married after the baby was born and were divorced six months later."

"That's..."

"Sad, I know. I feel bad for them."

"Wait." Caleb takes his glove off and walks toward me. His blue eyes are lit with marvel. "You feel bad for *them?* After what they did to you?"

"Yes. We were kids, they made a mistake—that doesn't mean I wanted anything but happiness for them both."

His stare bores into me, eyes still sparking. "You're amazing."

The words are whispered and then his mouth is on mine. This kiss is more passionate than our last as his hands cradle my face. He sets me at just the right angle, his tongue pressing against the seam of my lips, begging for entrance.

I grant it.

We kiss like we'll never kiss again. Our tongues run together, exploring, learning. My hands grip his waist as I pull him closer to me, wanting to feel his hard body against mine.

Our kiss grows more intense, his hands now roaming into my hair. He grips me harder, but soft enough that it doesn't hurt. The pressure feels good, feels right. Our bodies mesh together and when he rocks against me, I can feel the affect our connection is having on him. My hands dip under his shirt and up as I feel my way across his muscled back and around to his sculpted abs.

I begin to dip my hands into the front of his jeans but Caleb pulls away, his lips lingering on mine with a slow, lazy touch.

"We should probably stop before this goes any further and I'm not able to stop."

I jerk away from him, the reality of what we're doing setting in. I draw my hand to my mouth, touching the lingering tingle I feel there. I relish how good it feels.

"Caleb...w-we can't keep kissing like this."

"Why?"

"Excuse me?"

His eyes fall to slits. "Are you making up silly reasons in your head again? Before it was we couldn't be roommates because I used to date Delia, and now...oh shit." The proverbial light bulb goes off. "This is because of Delia, right? We can't kiss because of her and what happened in your past. You'd feel like your ex."

"In a way, yes."

"You're not him—*we're* not them. Delia and I are over. We've been over. There's nothing left there. I don't see the harm in moving on when she has too."

I straighten my back and meet his heated gaze head on. "Because it's so much more than that Caleb. You're her ex. I'm her best friend. There are just some lines you don't cross."

"Oh bullshit."

"Excuse me?"

"Did you fart? I said: bull...shit."

"Caleb—"

"I bet you could call Delia up right now and ask her if

she has a problem and she'd say no." He grins, and it's almost sinister. "As a matter of fact, I'll do it."

He reaches into his back pocket and I lunge at him like a lunatic, swatting at the phone in his hand.

"No! Caleb! Stop it right now!"

He snakes an arm around my waist and brings me in close to him. "Tell me then, Zoe. Tell me the real reason you don't want to do this."

My heart begins to work overtime with the way he's watching me. It's like he can see right through me, down to the very thread that holds me together.

I both love and hate how it makes me feel.

"I'm scared, Caleb. I don't want to like you. I don't want to do that Delia...but I can't help the attraction I feel toward you. You're like this magnetic field that's pulling me in. I don't know you well enough to decide if I want inside or if I want off the field."

He releases me and I take a step back, noticing when he slips his phone back into his pocket.

"How about this: let's be friends, no strings attached. If we kiss, we kiss. If something more comes of this, then it does, but I don't see why we should tiptoe around whatever this is for the sake of what-ifs."

"I..."

Can I do that? Can I just go with the flow on this? I'm usually so laid back about relationships and guys, but something with Caleb is different—and it goes beyond him and Delia.

I do want to get to know him better—as friends, as whatever.

"I can do that."

"*We* can do that."

"Just, like, don't make it weird."

He lets out a choked laugh. "Me? *I'm* gonna make it weird? Riiiight."

"Yep. You." I pick up my discarded glove, playing it cool, because we both know it would be me that made it weird before he did. "Now help me load this crap into my car. You're buying me lunch."

"OKAY, seriously, you are a stupid amazing cook."

Caleb lifts a shoulder, like the meal he just whipped up was no big deal. "I know."

"And you learned all that how exactly?"

"We had about three working channels, one being this old cooking station. That's where I learned a good portion of it. The rest was through trial and error."

"Trial and error? For *that*?"

"It's just a healthy spin on chicken Parmesan. It's not that hard to make."

I shake my head. "I'd have failed at the first step."

"Flattening chicken? You can't really mess that up..."

"Oh, trust me, I'd have found a way. And you learned all this in the...what did you say? The trailer park?"

He nods. "Yep. Born and raised."

Caleb goes to grab our empty plates, an attempt to change the subject—which I allow—but I swat his hand away.

"Nuh uh. I'll do that. You cooked, I'll clean."

"Fair enough."

I grab our plates and make my way to the sink, taking the time to rinse them clean before dropping them in the dishwasher. Piling the leftovers into a bowl, I slide it into the fridge. It's amazing that just a few weeks ago you would open it and only find milk, butter, eggs, and a few jars of salsa. Now it's stocked full of leftovers and all kinds of fresh groceries.

Grabbing my apron, I tie it around my waist and set about pulling out the ingredients to make brownies. Hey, he makes dinners, I make dessert—those are the rules.

I break an egg over a bowl and drop it in then turn to dump the shell in the trash, surprised to find a smiling Caleb still sitting at the counter.

"What?"

His grin grows, and he gives his head a shake. "Nothing. It's just cute to watch you flitter your way around the kitchen. I haven't had the chance to watch you bake yet. I'm usually only around to reap the rewards of your efforts, not watch the magic happen."

"What's so cute about it?"

"Everything. Your concentration, the way your tongue snakes out when you have to use the whisk..." He stalks my way and reaches out, brushing his finger against my cheek. "The speck of flour you have right here."

"That was *so* cliché."

"But you have to admit, it made your knees weak."

"Another cliché. You done yet?"

"Oh, baby, not even close."

I burst into laughter as Caleb swoops me into his arms, placing a kiss against my temple, shaking his head at me.

"You're something else, Caleb."

"You like it."

"You can't prove that."

His lips lift, and I know exactly what's running through his mind. "Oh, I can."

"You're going to kiss me again, aren't you?"

He responds by dipping his head and capturing my lips with his. His thumb sweeps across my cheek, his other hand gripping my waist and holding me close to him as his mouth moves over mine. His touch is gentle, sweet even.

We stand there wrapped together for who knows how long with our lips fused together.

It feels so good, so natural. It's only been hours since we agreed to be friends and see where this goes, but I can already feel the shift, and it worries me how good it feels.

"I need to finish making these brownies," I whisper when I pull my mouth from his.

"Yeah you do—I'm craving something sweet."

He winks; I nearly die laughing.

Caleb shakes his head and steps away from me. "I'll be on the couch while you calm down in here."

I wave him off and finish mixing the brownies, adding in a few chocolate chips for an extra rich batch.

I set the timer and slide dessert into the oven before slipping off my apron. I grab two beers from the fridge and make my way into the living room.

"Here." I hand Caleb one. "We have about twenty-five minutes."

"You want to watch something?"

"How about watch that dick disappear into this ass?"

He spits out the drink of beer he just took, his face red, laughter spilling out of him. "Holy fuck! Did you just ask me to do anal with you?"

I can't help but laugh along with him. "No, I just can't control the things that come out of my mouth sometimes."

"Because, I mean, I'm game if you are." He waggles his brows up and down.

"Keep dreaming, Caleb. Keep fucking dreaming."

"You're going to be so fun to live with." He grabs the remote from the table, still laughing. "You a fan of *It's Always Sunny in Philadelphia?*"

"Of what?"

"Just wait. You'll see."

We're not even five minutes into the first episode and my mouth has already dropped at least three times. I can see Caleb watching me out of the side of his eye.

"Right?"

"They're such train wrecks, but I can't look away."

"Just wait, it gets worse."

"Worse? That's possible?"

He chuckles. "Worse."

"Wow."

We finish out the episode and start the second before the timer goes off.

"Be right back," I tell him. "Pause it. I don't want to miss one second."

I race into the kitchen and use a toothpick to check the brownies. When it comes out clean, I remove them and set the pan on a rack to cool while we watch another episode or two.

"Okay, ready," I say, plopping back down on the couch.

When Caleb doesn't answer, I glance over at him.

He's asleep.

I went into the kitchen for two minutes and he fell asleep.

Poor guy.

Standing, I grab my beer bottle and his, dumping them both in the recycling bin before wrapping tin foil around the brownies. I'll have to take care of them in the morning.

"Mittens," I call quietly. "Bed time."

The small cat darts out from his favorite spot under the bar and races toward my bedroom. Guess you can say we've done this a few times.

I lean over the back of the couch and give Caleb a few shakes. "Hey, wakie wakie. Let's go to bed."

"Hmm?"

"Bed. Let's go."

"Like...together?"

"Together. You're sleeping with me tonight."

He gives me a crooked grin. "I don't think I'm up for it tonight, babe."

I laugh and give him another shake. "I meant *sleep* sleep. You're not sleeping on the floor, and no offense, but you're too big for the couch to be comfortable."

"My ass isn't *that* big."

I slap at said ass. "It's getting there."

He flips around quickly. "Did you just slap my ass?"

"Maybe. Did you like it?"

A shrug. "Maybe."

I give him a small laugh. "Come on. Bed."

We amble down the hallway. "I'm, uh, gonna go grab my stuff. You sure this is okay?"

"Yep. Now scoot. I'm getting sleepy."

Caleb heads to grab his pillow and blanket while I rush to clean up my painting supplies and try to make some sense of my messy bed.

I refuse to overthink this. I refuse to make this weird.

Caleb doesn't have a bed. He *has* to sleep in mine.

Right?

I climb into 'my side', which feels so weird because the

whole bed has always been my side, and then I wait for Caleb to make his move.

Unlike me, he doesn't hesitate. He dives right into the warmth, snuggling close to me.

"Oh my god," he moans, eyes closed, body wrapped tight in his blanket. "This is pure heaven."

"The bed or sleeping next to me?"

He smirks. "Maybe a little of both."

"Maybe?"

"Maybe a lot."

I laugh and reach over to turn off my bedside lamp before scooting down and making myself comfortable.

"Thank you, Zoe."

"For the bed?"

"For the bed, for the kisses, for the brownies I'll be eating for breakfast."

I lean over and place a kiss on his forehead. "Good night, Caleb."

"Good night."

CHAPTER 11

I HATE MYSELF.

I've been lying in bed for the past ten minutes trying to work up the courage to *not* text Caleb, because for some ungodly reason, I miss him.

Already.

And I've only been awake for thirty minutes.

I groan and throw my phone back to the end of the bed, refusing to give in.

I *want* to feel bad for liking him, for wanting to spend time with him, but it's so hard when he makes me feel the way he does. When he kisses me, my whole world is full of color. He makes me feel the way a blank canvas does: excited and nervous and ready for something new.

> Me: You ghosted again this morning. Is this going to be our thing now?

> Caleb: It's Sunday, remember? I have plans on Sundays.

> Me: Ah, yes. Your mysterious standing Sunday plans.

Caleb: It's not THAT mysterious. I go "home" on Sundays, make sure shit's straight.

Me: And home is in quotes because…

Caleb: Because it doesn't feel like home.

Caleb: Unlike your bed. ;-)

Me: You're trying to distract me with sexy talk.

Me: I'll allow it. Please continue.

Me: HOLD THE FUCKING PHONE

Caleb: *winces* You saw, huh?

Me: Oh, I fucking saw. ALL BUT TWO?

Caleb: They were REALLY good, so it's all your fault for being such an amazing, beautiful, generous, kind, sexy cook.

Me: What are you buttering me up for?

Me: Did you do something else?

Caleb: No. *bats lashes* I would never.

Me: I swear, if I walk to the fridge and I'm out of chocolate milk, a thunderous doom will rain down upon you.

Caleb: I'm so scared.

Me: As you should be! I'm scary as fuck without my chocolate milk.

Caleb: Glad I'm not there then.

Me: CALEB!

Me: UGH. Worst. Roommate. Ever.

Me: Wait, how'd you get "home"? Did you bus it?

Caleb: I did. It's only about two hours by bus. No biggie.

Me: I could have given you a ride.

Caleb: I'm used to it. I rode the bus even when I was able to ride my bike.

Me: But…why?

Caleb: It's just easier, safer. The ride out here can get a bit hairy.

Me: Fair enough.

Me: When will you be home? I'm already bored and you're missing Breakfast & Beats. I have some Tupac cranking right this moment.

Caleb: Now that I'm actually upset about.

Caleb: I should be home tonight, probably not until after midnight though. I take the last bus out whenever possible.

Me: Okay. Fine. I'll just be here.

Me: By myself.

Me: You know. Alone. By myself.

Caleb: I see someone's a bit of a drama bomb...

Caleb: Besides, Mittens is there. Snuggle with him.

Caleb: Also, it is ridiculous how you've pretty much stolen him from me. Don't think I didn't notice him sleeping at the end of your side last night. Total bullshit.

Me: What? I can't help it that I'm cuter than you and he loves me more.

Caleb: He loves you more? Maybe. Cuter? Don't push it.

Me: GASP!

Me: I'm WAY cute.

Caleb: You're sexy. That's a whole different level of cute.

Caleb: So…I have news.

Me: You've won the lottery and you're giving me one million dollars?

Caleb: Close.

Caleb: I have to extend my stay.

Me: That's not even kind of close.

Me: What's going on?

Caleb: Just some things I need to deal with. I should be home Tuesday night after study group.

Me: Tuesday?! Ughhhhhhh.

Caleb: I know, I know. Trust me, if I didn't HAVE to be here, I wouldn't. I hate this place.

Me: That bad?

Caleb: That FUCKING bad.

Me: Oh wow, you threw a cuss word in there. Okay, I believe you now.

Me: Don't worry, I'll take care of Mittens. He's going to fall even more in love with me though. Fair warning.

Caleb: Sigh. I figured as much. I might as well just sign over his adoption papers now.

Me: Nah. We can share him. I'm nice like that.

Me: I did a thing…

Me: DOWNLOAD ATTACHMENT

Caleb: You…you…

Caleb: YOU PUT A PINK AND PURPLE UNICORN SWEATER ON MY KITTEN?

Me: What? He LOVES it!

Caleb: I can see his disappointment from here.

Me: Nah, he's just mad right now because I won't let him push my pop off the table.

Caleb: Oh god. He loves doing that—
and sitting on your laptop. Don't let him
do that either.

Me: I've noticed he's keen on that.

Caleb: This one time, I had my laptop
balancing on the end of my bed. Shorts
were down to my knees, dick in my
hand, porn playing, and he comes and
sits RIGHT ON TOP OF MY
KEYBOARD. The sound kicks on and all
you can hear is LOUD AS FUCK
moaning. My roommates gave me shit
for days.

Me: First, I was not expecting a story
about you jerking off to porn. Second, I
think I love Mittens even more now.
YOU DO NOT WATCH PORN AND
SPANK YOUR MEAT WITH PEOPLE IN
THE HOUSE. The fuck is wrong
with you?

Caleb: When you get the urge, you get
the urge. Don't judge me.

Me: I'm not judging you…much.

Me: You're right. When there's an itch,
you gotta scratch it.

Me: JUST NOT WHEN OTHER PEOPLE
ARE HOME! GOSH!

Caleb: That tone…that was judgmental.

Me: You could hear my tone through text? Do you have a superpower I don't know about? Is that why you're so obsessed with comics? Because you have your own?

Me: Also…I'm not judging, I'm just not NOT judging you either. ;-)

Caleb: Yes, that's exactly why I read comics. You nailed me.

Me: Well, I haven't, but I could.

Caleb: Now THAT is how you flirt. I've taught you so well.

Me: Hush.

Me: Okay, for real though—why ARE you such a comic nerd? Is it the skintight, borderline sexy outfits?

Caleb: Totally. Have you seen the muscles on Superman? *fans self*

Caleb: But really, it was all I had as a kid. There was a comic shop a short bus ride away and I could pick up eight comics for like two bucks. Kept me entertained for weeks at a time.

Me: It's crazy to me how different your life there seems from your life here.

Caleb: Fresh start.

Caleb: College is the best thing to ever happen to me.

Me: Besides me, right?

Caleb: Sure, we'll go with that.

Me: CALEB! Tell me I am the best roommate you've ever had! You know it's true! Hell, I'm taking care of your damn cat for you.

Caleb: Because that is SUCH a hardship. *rolls eyes*

Me: That's not the point here.

Caleb: That is exactly the point here.

Caleb: Stop pretending to be upset. You know I adore you. Most days...

Me: Most days? MOST DAYS?!?

Caleb: I'm not changing my answer just because you caps lock me.

Me: INCORRIGIBLE!

Caleb: DOWNLOAD ATTACHMENT

Me: What is that?

Me: Is that you on a bus?! Are you on your way home a day early???

Caleb: Yep and yep.

Me: YAY!

Me: I mean, cool, whatever. Who gives a shit?

Caleb: You act like you've missed me or something.

Me: I AM DYING. I'm SO bored. Delia said this would happen too. That's why she was so adamant I get a new roomie. I followed her advice and look what's happened? I'm still bored because you're always gone.

Caleb: I'm the worst.

Me: I know.

Caleb: You're not even going to refute that? Not even to make me feel a bit better?

Me: No. Why should I? YOU SUCK.

Me: Kidding. Maybe.

Me: What do you want for dinner? My treat.

Caleb: Your treat as in you'll cook? Or your treat as in you'll buy?

Me: I feel like you want me to say buy because I'm a horrible cook.

Caleb: It would be the safest option, right?

Caleb: Actually, you know what? Let's cook together tonight. I'll teach you a few things.

Me: Okay, first…SO RUDE! Second, are you sure? That's a HUGE commitment.

Caleb: You cannot be THAT bad. We'll do something easy. Do you like Alfredo?

Me: Do I like Alfredo? Um, YES!

Caleb: We'll do that then. SUPER easy to make. You can't mess it up.

Me: We'll see…

Caleb: About thirty minutes out. You ready to cook?

Me: DOWNLOAD ATTACHMENT

Caleb: HOLY FUCKING SHIT.

Caleb: ARE YOU NAKED UNDER YOUR APRON?!

Me: WHAT? NO!

Me: Oh crap, it does look like I'm naked, huh? I just thought my boobs looked great in the shot and sent it.

Me: Don't forward that to your friends. ;-)

Caleb: Haha. Very funny. NOT.

Me: I thought it was hilarious.

Caleb: You're a real damn comedian.

Me: Oh hush, you grumpbutt. What do you want for dessert?

Caleb: Peanut butter cookies? With extra kisses. ;-)

Me: GAG.

Me: You're so corny sometimes.

Caleb: You enjoy it.

Me: Only never.

Caleb: LIES!

Caleb: Fifteen minutes.

Me: WAIT. How are you getting here from the bus station?

Caleb: Walking. It's only about two miles.

Me: Caleb...

Caleb: Zoe, I'll be fine. It'll be good exercise. I didn't get the chance to work out these last two days so I need it.

Me: Fine, but I'm only agreeing because you have one hot body and I know you like to keep it in shape.

Caleb: You think I'm hot, huh?

Me: Your body is hot.

Caleb: Which means I'M hot.

Me: No, it means your abs and your ass and your legs and your arms and your back and your jawline and your crooked nose and your stupid sexy full lips and your blue eyes and your hair that's in desperate need of a cut are hot. You're a whole different story.

Caleb: You make no sense.

Me: Personality, Caleb. Your personality is what makes YOU hot.

Caleb: So I AM hot? Or I'm not?

Me: You're sexy. That's a whole different level of hot. ;-)

Caleb: Oh. I see what you did there.

Caleb: Bus just stopped. I'll see you in about twenty.

CHAPTER 12

"I GET TO WHISK IT? Whisking is easy. I got this shit." I shove Caleb out of the way. "Move it. I'm a whisking pro, bro."

"You're proud of yourself for that, huh?"

"So proud," I tell him, whisking away at the creamy Alfredo sauce in the pan as he periodically pours in milk. "This cooking thing is easy so far."

"Yeah, you're not doing too bad. We only had to put out one small fire and start over twice. That's progress."

"Oh, I'm kicking ass and taking names. BAM!"

"Did you just Emeril that sauce?"

I give it another good whisk. "BAM! BAM!"

Caleb laughs. "You're not even doing it right."

"You're not right."

"Sure. Okay, I've turned the water on for the noodles. Watch that and finish out the sauce while I run up the street to grab garlic bread. You can't have Alfredo without garlic bread."

"Sticks—grab sticks. I like eating those more." He opens his mouth and I lift a finger his way. "Ah, ah, ah, not one dick joke, you got it?"

He tightens his lips, laughing to himself. "Yes, ma'am. You think you have everything under control?"

"Yep." I scan the recipe and directions on my phone. "It says add Parmesan and peppers."

"*Pepper*, like black pepper."

"Oh, well that makes more sense. Okay, so add *pepper* and then remove from heat when it reaches the consistency we'd like." I pause and grin his way. "I don't know about you, but I like it *thick*."

"And you said I couldn't make a dick joke? The shit is that?"

"I'm cuter than you, so I can do what I want."

He stalks toward me, chuckling. "Is that right?"

"Yep."

"Even in this apron of mine?"

Giving him a onceover, I screw up my lips, contemplating what he's offering. I gave him my apron that has a hand-painted portrait of Chris Hemsworth on it.

"Well...you *do* have Hemsworth on your apron, so that's giving you at least a few points." I push onto my tiptoes and lean into him. "But I'm still winning."

He places a gentle kiss on my cheek. "I'll just keep letting you believe that. Watch the food. I'll be back in ten minutes."

"Ten minutes?" It comes out a squeak.

"You can manage ten minutes on your own. You've been doing great so far."

"Yeah, because you've been here. That makes me relax and not panic."

"There's nothing to panic about. You're turning the sauce off and you're boiling water. You've boiled water plenty of times for your mac and cheese obsession. You got this."

"And if I burn the apartment down?"

He shrugs. "It's not my apartment."

"Hey! Is too!"

"Fine. I'll be mildly upset. There's a lot of money worth of comics in that bedroom."

"Plus Mittens."

"Well I was hoping in your haste to escape, you'd at least think to grab the cat."

"You're right. Good point."

Caleb grabs my keys off the counter. "You mind?"

"You remember how to drive, right?"

"I think I can manage a three-mile round trip."

"I hope so." I pat him on the shoulder twice as a good luck gesture. "I'd hate to have to chop off your nuts when I haven't yet had the chance to see them."

"If it's nuts you wanna see, baby…" He pretends to begin unbuttoning his pants.

I push at his chest, sending him closer to the door. "Get out of there. Out of my kitchen!"

He just laughs, shaking his head at me.

"PLEASE DON'T BE mad at me!"

Caleb pauses in the doorway, one hand still on the knob, the other holding a paper bag. "That's never a good thing to hear."

"I know, I know, but you have to understand, this is kind of your fault."

"My fault?" He sniffs at the air. "What's that smell? What did you do, Zoe?"

I hold out my hands, trying to defend myself against his words. "You're the one who said I would be just fine on my own for ten minutes. You were right, but Caleb? You were gone for twelve."

His eyes widen as he makes his way into the kitchen, sets the bag on the counter, and peers into the pot on the stove.

"Am I looking at what I think I'm looking at?"

"Y-Yes."

"That's the sauce we worked on?"

"Uh, yes. Yes it is."

He tips his head to the side. "How?"

"Um...how?"

"Yes. How?"

"It just happened."

Caleb barely manages to suppress a shocked laugh.

"Just happened? The sauce magically conformed to the pan and turned brown?"

I nod and wiggle my fingers. "Magic."

"Mmhmm. And the water?"

"Th-The what?"

"The water? For the noodles?"

My mouth drops open. "Oh."

"Oh? What does 'oh' mean?"

"I forgot."

His head whips toward the pot that *used* to hold the water for the noodles, just in time to catch smoke billowing out from underneath it.

Rushing into action, he grabs the pot and switches off the burner before a fire can catch. He takes the pot to the sink, running water over it to cool it off before refilling it and setting it on a new burner.

He points at it. "No touchy touchy."

"But...but..." My shoulders sag in defeat. "Fine, but I didn't catch it on fire! That's an improvement!"

He regards me with an amused smile. "You turned our nearly done sauce brown and you boiled an entire pot of water until it was empty. Within ten"—I open my mouth to correct him and he holds a hand up—"sorry, twelve minutes. You are officially fired from cooking tonight."

"And the cookies?"

"I said cooking. You can still bake. You're somehow actually good at that."

"It's because there are directions and timers and love involved. Baking is a labor of love!"

"Okay, grandma, calm down. I'll remake the sauce, but you need to keep your distance. I don't know what kind of voodoo you're up to, but there will be none of that in my kitchen."

I hang my head, feeling a little embarrassed about my flub. "Okay, I get it, I suck."

"You don't suck."

I can't not make the comment… "Oh, but I do," I say, winking.

He breaks out in laughter and grabs the bag he brought home, pulling out the package of breadsticks and shaking it. "Can you manage putting these on a pan?"

I narrow my eyes at him. "Yes, you ass."

"Hey, I have valid reasons for questioning your cooking skills. All I asked you to do was watch water boil and move a saucepan from one burner to another."

"A watched pot never boils," I mutter.

"What was that?"

"I said the water wouldn't boil. I was watching and watching, and nothing was happening, so I turned up the heat and starting working on the cookie dough."

"And then what happened?" he pushes.

"I forgot."

"You forgot?"

"That's what I said."

He drops his head, and I can see his shoulders shaking.

I toss a hand towel at him, barely missing the stove—and another fire. "Stop laughing! This is a serious problem!"

"This is why I am so confused on how you can bake, but not cook."

"Timers, man! Timers make all the difference."

"I am so happy I moved in so you're not dying of starvation or cursing me in ten years when all that mac and cheese is sitting on your hips."

"They'd be the happiest hips in the world. Mac and cheese is goddamn delicious, and you know it."

He grabs the sauce ingredients from the fridge...for the third time tonight. "Homemade mac and cheese is delicious. That boxed crap is shit, and you know it."

"You have me there."

The timer sounds on the oven so I grab an oven mitt, shove Caleb aside, and pull dessert out before switching it off. I place them on a cooling rack and turn to my baking cabinet, looking for Kisses to put on top of the cookies.

"Shit," I mutter when I find my almost empty bag. I spin around, showing Caleb what I find. "Looks like you're getting about four Kisses tonight."

He grins, grabbing the paper bag he brought home off the counter and pulling out a brand new package. "Oh, I'm getting more than four." Leaning against the counter, he crosses his legs, tossing the bag of chocolates from one hand to the other, back and forth. "How about this: you get one Kiss for every two I get."

I cross my arms over my chest and mirror his pose. "One for one."

"One for two."

"One for one."

"One for three," he counters.

"One for two."

A victorious grin spreads over his lips and I realize I just fell right into his trap.

"Dammit," I groan. "Ass."

"Hey, I won fair and square. It's not my fault you suck at cooking *and* negotiating."

An idea hits me, and I sashay toward him like he's my prey. I slide up close to him, batting my lashes and bringing my lips within an inch of his, my hands resting on his solid chest.

"You're right. You did win," I whisper huskily.

My nearness is influencing him. It's obvious in the way his chest begins to rapidly move up and down, the way his body cants toward me, his eyes dilating.

He's teetering on the edge of excitement, and I know just what will make him tip over.

I slowly run my hands down his chest, over his abs, and rest them on the waistband of his jeans. I peek up at him. "But you didn't say *where* I had to kiss you."

I move just left of his lips and place a gentle kiss on his skin, and then another directly beneath it...and one more just along his jawline before pressing my lips to his neck. He sucks in a deep breath, his hips jutting out to make any sort of contact they can. His hands land on my waist, holding me close.

I continue to pepper kisses all the way up to his ear, relishing the way his body reacts when I reach the spot just behind it. An obvious shudder runs through him and his hips press my away again.

I trace a path all the way to the other side, eliciting the same reaction there.

My kisses continue until my lips have touched every inch of his face. He stands there accepting them, eyes closed and gasping for air, arousal clear as day.

When I settle the last kiss in the same place I started, he sighs and rests his forehead against mine. Hands tighten on my waist, and I'm sure I'll be bearing an imprint even tomorrow.

"Zoe?" he says breathlessly.

"Yeah?"

"Move."

"Huh?"

"You need to move or I'm going to kiss you like you've never been kissed before. I'm going to run my hands all over your body until you're writhing beneath me in absolute want. Then I'll devour you, and I don't think either of us are ready to take that step just yet." He swallows thickly. "So, please...move."

I step away from him as he exhales a shaky breath and pushes past me.

"Start the breadsticks and watch the water. I'm taking a cold shower."

I can't help the laugh that escapes me, and it grows when I hear him mutter a "dammit" before the bathroom door slams closed.

I don't know what's worse: that I want him to devour me, or that I'd let him.

Caleb Mills is going to be the death of me.

"FEELING BETTER?" I ask when he emerges fifteen minutes later.

He scrubs his hair with a towel and glowers my way. "You are an evil, evil woman, Zoe Williams."

I lift a shoulder. "You're the one who played dirty first, Caleb. Fair's fair."

"Yeah, but I didn't get *that* dirty."

"Uh huh. Now, check it out." I wave a hand over the stove. "I didn't ruin anything this time. Breadsticks are cooking and the water is boiling."

"Wow, I'm impressed. I'll whip up the sauce real quick and then we should be in business. I'm starving all of a sudden."

"Were you masturbating in there?"

"What? No!" he says too quickly.

"That was not convincing at all. You totally jerked off in the shower just now."

"I-I did no such th-thing." His voices wavers at the end.

"You are a terrible liar."

"I was in the shower for like fifteen minutes. What kind of man do you think I am?"

"Obviously a very speedy one."

He rushes toward me, giving me a lazy grin. "Oh I'll show you speedy."

"All right." I push at his chest. "Back it up, bucko. We have dinner to finish up."

Caleb gives me an exaggerated eye roll. "You're no fun sometimes."

"I'll show you fun later."

"Is that a promise or..."

"It's a *we'll see.*"

"Come on, Zoe." He waggles his brows. "You can't resist this sexy body much longer."

"I can, and I will."

Now that he's mentioned it, I realize this is probably the longest I've ever gone without sleeping with someone, especially with someone I've been...well, whatever I've been doing with Caleb.

We've been doing this tango of flirting for weeks now, sometimes in person and sometimes by text, but in this day and age, that doesn't matter much anymore. Flirting is flirting no matter if it's through a screen or not. It progresses the relationship like it never used to before.

Point is, we have something going on, and we're clearly still tiptoeing around the end game of it all.

It's like we're stuck at bat waiting for the perfect pitch, the perfect moment.

Caleb can joke all he wants about me being the one waiting to make the final move, but truth is, we're both too scared to push this any further. He says he's over Delia, and I believe him about that, but I don't think he's too keen on jumping into bed with her best friend so soon. He's not that kind of guy, and he's never been that kind of guy.

It's what I like about him so much: he gives a shit. He doesn't jump into bed with anyone. He has to care about them. They have to mean something to him.

That is so opposite of what I've always done and what the men I've been with have always done.

For the first time in my life, I'm being cautious.

And I'm loving the slow build.

Though we make no sense together—the artist and the athlete—we somehow make two worlds collide in the best of ways.

"Whatever you say," he mutters, not sounding convinced at all.

I don't think I'm convinced either.

He moves around the kitchen, finishing up dinner. He pops the oven open to check on the breadsticks and pauses for a beat too long.

"Zoe?" The way he says it, like something is wrong, has me gripping the edges of the counter.

"Y-Yes?" My response is full of caution and worry.

"Did you happen to turn the oven on?"

I drop my head into my hands, covering my face in shame. "Shit." He laughs and gathers me into his arms, pressing a kiss against my temple. "I told you I was bad at this."

"Let's just be thankful you can bake."

"We make quite the pair, huh? You do all the cooking, I do all the baking."

He stiffens ever so slightly, and I hear him gulp. "Yeah. Yeah we do."

Caleb: I hear sappy music coming from your room. Should I be worried?

Me: Nah. I'm painting. I have a huge project due next week. I'll probably be holed up in here for hours at time until then.

Caleb: Well can't you put something good on?

Me: Good? GOOD? Joy Division is the epitome of good!

Caleb: Joy Division makes me want to rock in a corner with my thumb in my mouth.

Caleb: What about something from your infamous Breakfast & Beats I've yet to be able to participate in?

Me: No. You don't paint to DMX or Tupac or Nas or Ice Cube. Or Color Me Badd.

Caleb: You actually listen to Color Me Badd?

Me: What? I Wanna Sex You Up is a classic!

Caleb: Hey, Zoe?

Me: Yeah?

Caleb: I wanna TEXT you up. ;-)

Me: I hate you for that.

Caleb: You liar.

Caleb: Now please, change the music. I won't come in there and force you because it's your zone and your space and whatever, but I will beg, and I will beg A LOT. I have nothing but free time right now.

Me: You do not have free time. You're studying.

Caleb: And how do you know that?

Me: Because you're studious and responsible, that's how.

Caleb: Whatever. Change the music. No emo shit.

Me: But the emo shit is what you're supposed to paint to. It brings out the emotions of the colors.

Caleb: Fine. Anything but Joy Division then.

Me: The Smiths? The Cure?

Caleb: ...No. That's basically the same thing.

Me: Then what?

Caleb: Can't you put on something less...sad?

Me: Hmm...

Me: One moment.

Me: This better?

Caleb: FUCK YES!

Caleb: Zeppelin is always the answer.

Me: What about Pink Floyd?

Caleb: That works too.

Me: WHAT! They are the EPITOME of sad music!

Caleb: It's all about perspective, baby.

Me: You're just saying that because you hate Joy Division.

Caleb: My lips are sealed.

Me: Hate you.

Caleb: Liar.

Caleb: I have bad news.

Me: Last time you told me that you didn't come home for DAYS.

Caleb: It was not DAYS, and I ended up coming home early.

Me: Semantics.

Me: What's the news?

Caleb: Wellllll…

Me: Caleb!

Caleb: Fine. Remember that date we're supposed to go on?

Me: The Rocky Horror Picture Show. I remember everything. Continue.

Caleb: Yeah…remember how you talked me out of rage-quitting because they scheduled me to work the night of the show?

Me: Yes…

Caleb: I can't get anyone to cover my shift. I'm stuck with it.

Me: You can't go.

Caleb: Correct.

Me: WHAT. UGH! This is so not cool!

Caleb: I know. I'm bummed.

Me: You are not. You didn't even want to see it once you learned it's a musical.

Caleb: Not true. The idea has been growing on me. I want to know what all this toast throwing is about and why I need to "do the time warp"…whatever the fuck that is.

Me: It's just a jump to the left…

Me: LOLOLOLOL

Caleb: *stares*

Me: That was REALLY funny if you've actually seen it! Give me SOME credit.

Caleb: No. Anyway, yeah, I can't go.

Me: But the next showing isn't until next month.

Caleb: Then we'll go then.

Me: But you'll probably hate me and move out by then.

Caleb: Nonsense!

Caleb: Well...maybe. ;-)

Me: HEY! WATCH IT!

Caleb: I kid, I kid. I'll never tire of your delicious desserts.

Me: Or my sparkling personality. Or my ass. Or my small yet magnificent rack. Or my gorgeous hazel eyes, luscious locks, and loooooong tan (AND TONED!) legs. Or my kisses.

Caleb: Are you done rambling on about how sexy you are?

Me: *reads back through what I wrote* Yep. Covered it all.

Caleb: So full of yourself.

Me: Hey, if I don't love me, who will?

Caleb: That's an excellent point.

Caleb: Hey, Zoe?

Me: Yeah?

Caleb: I'm really sorry I can't make the movie this month, but I promise I'll be around for it next month.

Me: Swear?

Caleb: On my entire comic book collection.

Me: I'm holding you to that.

Me: And selling it if you back out.

Caleb: Evil.

Me: Are you coming home tonight?

Caleb: Yes, but it won't be until late.

Me: Does this mean I'm on my own for dinner?

Caleb: Yes, this means you can have cereal for dinner.

Me: You know me so well.

Me: Also, I really feel like I'm getting the shaft here.

Caleb: I can give you the shaft…

Me: I walked right into that one, huh?

Caleb: Oh yeah.

Caleb: Why are you getting the shaft?
And if not from me, who are you getting
it from?

Me: Oh you ARE the one shafting me.
You moved in and promised to make me
ALLLL the dinners if I made desserts.
You, sir, are a liar. I bust my ass over a
hot oven to cook you pies and cookies
and cupcakes, and what do I get?
CEREAL!

Caleb: To be fair, if I didn't live there,
you'd still be eating cereal, so are you
REALLY getting that shafted on this
whole deal?

Me: Yes. You're shafting me hard.

Caleb: Okay, now you're the one being
dirty with the shafting.

Me: What if I like it dirty?

Caleb: Zoe…it's not nice to tease.

Me: I'm not teasing.

Me: Or am I? ;-)

Caleb: Oh you are, and there's nothing I can do about it because I'm not there because I'm stuck at this stupid, obnoxious, no help of a study group while you go on and on about being shafted and liking it dirty. That's teasing.

Me: You're right. I'm sorry.

Caleb: Is it sad that I know you just typed that with the wickedest grin on your face? Because you did, didn't you?

Me: Maybe...

Me: Yes.

Me: DOWNLOAD ATTACHMENT

Me: By the way, Mittens says he misses you.

Caleb: Dammit, Zoe, did you buy him ANOTHER new sweater?

Me: What? He looks so stinkin' cute in them, and this one looks like a sweater vest. He looks so smart and sophisticated.

Caleb: That poor, poor cat.

Me: Right? His dad keeps abandoning him. ;-)

Caleb: Not on purpose!

Caleb: But do you see why I wanted to move in with you? My old roommates wouldn't have paid him any attention at all. At least now I know someone's showing him affection.

Me: THAT'S why you wanted to move in? So I can be your built-in cat sitter?

Caleb: That and your ass.

Me: Right? It's so great, isn't it?

Caleb: Omg. I'm going to go do something productive before you start going on about your attributes again.

Me: Don't be jealous because I'm sexier than you, Caleb.

Caleb: You are, Zoe. You so are.

Me: What are you doing tomorrow morning?

Caleb: Why?

Me: Reasons.

Caleb: I was going to sleep in a bit since I only have afternoon class.

Me: Excellent! My morning class was canceled. Breakfast & Beats—it's happening. Ten AM. Be there or be the biggest L-7 weenie on the block.

Caleb: Okay. Yep. I have a homer.

Me: A homer?

Caleb: BONER. I HAVE A BONER. MY GODDAMN DICK IS HARD.

Me: And what brought this on?

Caleb: A hot chick quoted my second favorite movie to me. Instant hard-on.

Me: Ah, yes. I forgot about your love for The Sandlot.

Me: Want me to say something else?

Caleb: NO!

Me: Why?

Caleb: Because it's going to be real awkward next time I'm watching it and I get a boner remembering you saying it.

Me: Hmm, fair enough.

Me: But B&B? You in?

Caleb: I'm in. I've heard too much about it to skip this.

Caleb: And fair warning, my expectations are high. You better deliver on not only breakfast, but beats too.

Caleb: Dancing too. I wanna see that ass shake.

Me: You're on.

"...*GIVE IT TO YA*."

"Please. Stop. I am begging you."

"Excuse me." I pause mid-booty shake. "You're the one who said you wanted to see this ass shake."

I continue gyrating, swinging my hips in circles before letting my arms loose and giving my whole body a shake. All the while I stare Caleb down, a smirk on my lips.

He's hating this, and I'm loving every minute of it.

"I did, and that was my mistake, which I am very, *very* sorry for making."

"That's just mean, Caleb."

"And true. We cannot forget how true it is." He wraps

an arm around my waist and pulls me into his arms, landing a kiss on my neck. "You are a horrible singer *and* dancer." His lips find my ear. "But you're still sexy as hell."

I attempt to wrestle away from him, swatting at his hands with the spatula I'm holding. "If you don't let me go, I'm going to burn breakfast."

"Fine, fine." He releases me and steps away. "The floor is yours, Chef Zoe."

I point the spatula his way as I walk backward to the stove. "You are a smartass this morning—a *mean* smartass."

"Hey, I'm just sayin', we don't want you breaking your stellar no-burnt-eggs-and-bacon track record...even though you are cheating with the bacon."

"Oh my gosh, I am *not* cheating! It's still bacon, isn't it?"

"Pre-cooked bacon, Zoe. Pre-cooked."

"You really want to trust *me* to fry bacon?"

"You can always put it in the oven. That requires no skill." He winks at me. "And you can even use your favorite thing: a timer."

"You can put bacon in the oven?"

"Yes? Did you not know that?"

"I...I thought you were supposed to fry it. My whole life has been a lie."

He chuckles at me. "Next time we have Breakfast and Beats, I'll show you."

I flip the eggs in the pan, shaking my head. "My mind is blown right now, Caleb, completely blown. My life is about to change. I can have real bacon again."

He snaps his fingers. "Ha! Even you know it tastes different!"

I roll my eyes even though he can't see me. "*Everyone* knows it tastes different. It's simply the price you pay for convenience and those extra five to ten minutes of sleep in the morning."

"I don't think I can argue there. I do love me some sleep."

"But you never get enough. You're always on the go." I move the eggs onto a plate and grab a few pieces of bacon that have been slowly heating in another pan, sliding those onto the plate. I carry it over to Caleb and pin him with a stern stare. "Hence why you're missing our Rocky Horror date tonight. Jerk."

"Thank you," he says, picking up the hot sauce he got out and pouring it over his eggs. "You're still going?"

"Of course."

"Even without me?"

I make my way back over to the stove and crack two eggs for myself. "I've always gone without you. It's a monthly showing and I haven't missed one yet."

"No shit?"

"Yep, and just because you're ditching our date doesn't mean I'm ditching it."

"I am not ditching. I tried to pull every string I have but I can't find anyone who'll cover the shift for me."

"Uh huh. You just hate me."

"Your singing and dancing? Maybe. Hate you? Never." I hear his fork scrape against his plate. "These are really good, by the way. I'll make a chef out of you yet."

I turn to him and lift a brow. "Hey, I've always been able to make bacon and eggs. I didn't need your help for that one."

"No, you're right. You just needed my help boiling water, right?"

I go to grab a towel off the counter to throw at him when he lets out a yelp.

"Ow! You little shit!"

Just then, Mittens runs out from his favorite spot at the bar and over to me.

"Oh really?" Caleb's eyes are bright with laughter as he grabs his plate and takes it to the sink. "You've turned my own cat against me, huh? I talk a little bit of shit and he bites me? That's so messed up, Zoe."

I scoop Mittens into my arms and give him a snuggle. "That's a good little buddy," I whisper to him. Then I stick my tongue out at Caleb. "Serves you right for being a jerk."

He presses a kiss to my cheek and ruffles Mitten's head.

"You." The grin he gives me makes my knees knock

together. Such a simple word, and yet it's filled to the brim with affection.

Caleb's smitten with me, and I can sure as hell tell him the feeling is mutual.

CHAPTER 14

"COMING!"

"That's what she said!" I holler back through the door.

Delia swings it open. "You did not just say that."

"I did."

She lifts her eyes skyward and waves me inside. "Get the hell in here and hug me, you brat. I haven't seen you since I moved out. What gives?"

I step inside her and Zach's home and wrap my arms around her. It's been weeks since I saw her last, but we've still talked nearly every day. "I've been busy."

She releases me and gives me a look. "Bull."

"Fine. I wanted to give you a little bit of space with the move, honeymoon period and all that. There was a little bit of sulking and then dealing with my new roomie."

She gives me a grin as I follow her into the living room. She settles down on the couch and wraps her blanket around her, patting the spot next to her. "Sit and spill. We'll put something on for background noise and have a glass of wine while we gab."

"Gab? We don't *gab*, Delia."

"Well we do now, dammit. I miss girl talk with you. I

love Zach like crazy, but I need a little estrogen in my life right now. Tell me all about life without me and what it's like living with Caleb."

My stomach rolls when she says his name.

Caleb...the reason I'm here.

It's time to tell her how I'm feeling, because every single day, I can feel myself liking him more and more. I can't let this keep heading in the direction it is without Delia knowing.

"Wine is exactly what I need."

There must be something about the way I say it, because Delia raises her brows my way before she pushes herself off the couch and into the kitchen.

"So how are things, Zoe?"

"Things are...interesting."

She grabs two glasses from the cabinets before heading toward the fridge. "Huh. Interesting how?"

"In a lot of ways."

Delia returns to the couch, setting down the cups and a fresh bottle of white wine. She sits forward and pours us both a glass then hands me mine.

She curls her legs underneath her and takes a sip, regarding me a moment, knowing something's up. I try my best not to make eye contact.

"What kind of ways?"

Fucking hell.

I down my entire glass of wine and nearly slam it back down on the table.

"I like Caleb." It comes out in one rushed breath.

"You like him?" she says calmly, swirling her wine in her glass.

"Yes."

"Like...how?"

"I *like* him."

"Oh," she says.

"Yep."

"Is that why our conversations have been feeling...rushed?"

"Yes!" I nearly explode. "It's so hard to talk to you when I feel like I've been hiding something."

"You know that's okay, right? To have a crush on him? I'm not going to be mad." She lifts a shoulder and takes another sip. "He's a good-looking guy. Can't blame you there."

I drop my head into my hands. "It's more than that, Delia."

"More?"

"More. He's the first person I think about in the morning. I rush to check my phone when it pings. I *want* to be near him and miss him when he's away. I *like* him."

She purses her lips, swirling the wine glass again. "Huh."

"We, uh, we..."

"Spit it out."

"We've kissed. A lot."

She studies me, not saying a word.

I feel like the world's shittiest friend. I mean who goes around kissing their bestie's ex-boyfriend? What kind of friend does that?

"I'm sorry, Delia. I'm so sorry. I'm a horrible friend, but I couldn't help it. He's just so...*Caleb*. He's hot and kind of annoying and so kind." I groan and shake my head, dropping it into my hands to hide. "*So* fucking kind. He works himself to the bone and wants to make something out of his life so badly, wants to better himself, but he doesn't realize he's already an amazing guy. Plus, you know...that body."

My breath is coming out all shaky and I feel like I'm rambling, but I'm so scared to face her, to see her reaction. I don't want her to hate me for this. I can't help my feelings any more then Caleb can.

"I just...I like him, Delia. I like him so fucking much, and I hate myself for it."

Delia bursts into laughter.

Slowly, I lift my head and glance her way. Her head is thrown back and her body is shaking.

"Wha..."

She fans her hand in front of her face, trying to calm herself. She downs the rest of her wine and sets the now empty glass on the table before facing me. Sticking out her hands, she beckons for mine. I mirror her pose and tentatively place my hands in hers.

"Zoe, it's okay."

"What?"

"It is okay. There's no reason for you to hate yourself. It's fine. *I'm* fine with it. In fact, I'm delighted to hear this."

My mouth drops open, shocked by what I'm hearing. "You're what?"

"I'm happy as hell. Besides Zach, you're my most favorite person in this entire world, and Caleb's probably my third. Why wouldn't I want my favorite people to find happiness?"

"But he's your ex-boyfriend."

"I know."

"Delia, he's *your* fucking *ex-boyfriend!*"

"You keep saying that like I wasn't the one who dated him for six months."

My lips quirk up. "Caleb said almost the exact same thing to me once."

"That does not surprise me." She squeezes my hand. "Zoe, if you like Caleb and he makes you happy, then go for it. He's a great guy and I think he could be good for you."

"Delia..."

"Hey, look at me." I meet her eyes. "No weirdness from me, I promise. I'm madly in love with the giant pain in the ass in the basement. There's no jealousy or resentment or anything like that. I want you to feel what I feel with Zach, and if it's Caleb who makes you feel that way, then it's him. Caleb and I were never going to make it. We had a surface-level relationship. There were no fireworks in the sky when it came to us. We just were. It was more convenient than anything else—not that he wasn't a good guy or that I didn't care for him, I just didn't care for him like I should have, if that makes sense."

I nod. "It does, because I care for him like I should."

"Well that's already an improvement over your past relationships."

"I feel like I should be offended by that, but you're totally right." All at once, so many emotions hit me, and tears begin to brim in my eyes. I blink them away before they can fall. "We're not at the same level you and Zach are at, but I do like him a lot. I think whatever it is that's going on between us has potential."

"Like long term? Not one of your flings?"

"He doesn't feel like a fling."

"Can I ask..."

She doesn't even have to voice the question. "We haven't slept together. For one, I couldn't do that to you, and two, I'm not ready for that step yet."

"But now that I've given you my blessing..."

"Oh, it's going down now."

She laughs and wipes at her own tears. "There's my girl."

More wine is poured into her glass. She shakes the bottle my way, but I decline. "Driving," I tell her.

"Right. So how are things in the roommate department? You know, other than you wanting to get down and dirty with him."

"They aren't bad. He spent a lot of the first couple

weeks being gone all the time, but things are settling and now he's home a lot more. That part has been amazing."

"And the bad parts?"

"He uses all my body wash and he always conveniently forgets to wear shirts. Oh, and he cockblocked me the first night we went out."

"Back up—why were you on the prowl if you have the hots for Caleb?"

"Well, I wasn't on the prowl, but an opportunity arose, and he deemed it his duty to make sure I didn't go home with anyone but him."

"That so?"

"Yep. That was the first night we kissed."

"And has it progressed since then?"

"Emotionally? Sort of. I mean, I like him more than I did that night, but I'm scared, you know?"

"Scared of what?" she asks. "Of Caleb?"

"Not like *of* him, more of what he makes me feel, makes me want...something stable and normal." I send her an accusatory glare. "This is all your fault."

"Mine?" She reels back. "What in the hell did I do?"

"You had to go and fall in love and shit. Seeing you and Zach together made me all mushy inside. I've had a horrible track record with dudes, and that's why I've always been more of a friends with benefits kind of girl, but ever since you got all googly-eyed over Zach, I've wanted more for myself. I want what you two have."

"I want that for you too, Zoe. It's the most amazing and infuriating feeling in the world."

"Infuriating?"

"Well, at least with Zach. Dude is exhausting sometimes."

"You know I can hear you two, right?" His voice trails up the stairs leading to the basement.

"Quit eavesdropping, you turd!"

"Quit talking so loud, you really good best friend!"

Delia gets that goofy grin across her face again. "See? He's impossible."

"He's a good guy."

"He knows!" Zach calls.

I ignore him and continue. "And he's not wrong. You really are a good best friend, Delia, like the best of the best. Someone needs to get you a trophy."

"Oh, a trophy! I like shiny things." She claps her hands together. "But in all seriousness, Zoe, I don't think you have anything to be afraid of. When you fall in love—"

I hold my hand up to stop her. "Hey now, no one said anything about falling in love."

She mutters something. "Fine. When you really like someone, and the universe or fate or whatever you want to call it says you two go together like cheese and bread—"

"Uh, what?"

"Grilled cheese. Keep up."

"Right, right. Continue," I tell her.

"Then everything will work out. You'll have your 'aha

moment'. Things will start making sense and you'll start feeling a whole lot less scared about what lies ahead. So just let it ride, you know? See where this thing with Caleb takes you. Have your moment, Zoe. You deserve it."

I have the urge to bite at my nails, which isn't something I've done since I was a little kid, but my insides are all twisted right now. What Delia's saying is making sense.

I just have to see where this takes me, see if there's a future with Caleb, and that's something I won't know until I give him a shot, give *us* a shot.

I take a deep breath and let it out. "You're right. You are definitely right. You sure you're—"

"I swear, if you ask me if I'm okay with this one more damn time," she warns.

"Fine, fine. Message received."

"Good." She gives me a warm, genuine smile. "I'm really happy for you, Zoe."

"Yeah?" She nods. I sit back on the couch for the first time since arriving, finally feeling relaxed and almost ready to take on the world. "Good. Me too."

CHAPTER 15

Me: Question.

Caleb: Answer…maybe.

Me: What are you doing for spring break?

Caleb: Is that still a thing?

Me: Um, YES. Now answer me.

Caleb: Nothing? Because I didn't think that was still a thing.

Me: How do you not know that's still a thing?! You're in college!

Caleb: Well if you're talking like, you know, going to the beach and being all spring break-y, then I did not know that was still a thing.

Me: I'm talking just taking the week off.

Caleb: Pose your follow-up question then.

Me: Me + you + Outer Banks = fun?

Caleb: One, OBX is EXPENSIVE AS SHIT. Two, please see my first response.

Me: HA! That's where I have you. My parents actually live in OBX. Free room and board.

Caleb: So we're spending spring break with your parents?

Me: Nah. They'll be out of town visiting my grandma. We'd have the place to ourselves most of the time. What do you say?

Caleb: What exactly does "most of the time" mean?

Me: They'll be there for the first day, but they are leaving super early the next morning.

Caleb: I HAVE TO MEET YOUR PARENTS?!

Caleb: Why does that make me so nervous?

Me: It shouldn't. They'll love you.

Caleb: Are they cool with you living with a dude?

Me: YOU'RE A GUY?!

Me: Yes, you loser. They trust me, but my dad did threaten to cut your nuts off if you tried to "get fresh" with me.

Caleb: He said that? Get fresh?

Me: I love that it's THAT part you focus on and not the potential harm to your nuts.

Caleb: Only because I know they're safe. I'm not that kind of guy.

Me: Fair point.

Me: So, you in?

Caleb: I'll have to put in the time off of work…

Me: Don't forget to mention you're not above pimping yourself out.

Caleb: YOU'RE not above pimping me out. I am.

Me: Semantics.

Me: I'm tired. Help me stay awake.

Caleb: DOWNLOAD ATTACHMENT

Me: Wow, a picture of our living room. How neat.

Caleb: Look closer.

Me: Omg. Dying. Why is he hiding under the couch?

Caleb: Because I sat on the remote and accidentally turned the volume up REALLY high during a loud scene and he just took off scared as shit. Now he won't come out.

Me: Aww…I feel so bad for him.

Caleb: DOWNLOAD ATTACHMENT

Caleb: Did I mention he was sitting on my stomach when it happened?

Me: That's a tiny scratch. You just wanted to send me a picture of your abs.

Caleb: Guilty.

Caleb: Aren't you supposed to be working right now?

Me: I am…kind of. We're dead tonight, so I'm bored. That's what happens when it's a slow movie release week— no one here wanting to dine and watch.

Me: I wish they'd just cut me already.

Caleb: That'd be nice. Then you could come tend to my wound.

Me: There's a box of Disney Princess Band-Aids in my bathroom in the medicine cabinet. #nurseout

Caleb: Your bedside manner needs a lot of work.

Me: Opinions are like assholes, Caleb.

Caleb: Sassy AND mean tonight. Noted.

Caleb: Keep it up and I'll make you sleep on the couch.

Me: Did you just threaten to kick me out of my own bed?

Caleb: It's OUR bed.

Me: No, that is MY bed. I just let you sleep in it.

Me: Speaking of, we really need to get you your own. I'm tired of waking up to the smell of your farts in the middle of the night.

Caleb: Those are YOUR farts waking you up. Trust me, they wake me up too.

Me: I hate you.

Caleb: You can't.

Me: I can, and I do.

Caleb: You can't, and you don't.

Caleb: Now come home already. I'm getting bored myself. I've already watched three movies and started and stopped two shows.

Me: So you've been a bum on the couch all day.

Caleb: Hey, I get like one good day off every couple weeks. I'll be lazy when I can be lazy.

Me: Okay, okay. You got me there. I'll allow it.

Caleb: *rolls eyes* I'm SO glad I have your permission to relax.

Me: Yeah, me too.

Caleb: DOWNLOAD ATTACHMENT

Me: Is that your masturbating hand?

Caleb: Well, yes.

Caleb: But it's also my right hand...

Me: Cool?

Me: WAIT.

Me: You got your brace off! YAY!

Caleb: Kind of. I have to do physical therapy.

Me: Seriously? Well that part blows.

Caleb: Tell me about it.

Me: What did we learn from all of this?

Caleb: Fracturing your hand isn't a good idea.

Me: True. And what else?

Caleb: I know you want me to say not to fight, but it was a necessary evil.

Me: Are you ever going to tell me the story?

Caleb: You don't want to hear this tale.

Me: You don't get to tell me what I do and don't want, Caleb.

Me: YOU'RE NOT MY REAL DAD.

Caleb: You're right. That'd make this whole us-making-out-all-the-time thing pretty awkward.

Me: And gross. Let's not forget gross.

Caleb: I thought that was obvious.

Me: It is.

Me: But Caleb? I'd really like to hear the story some time. Even if it's a sordid tale, I want to know more about you. I want to learn about your past and your aspirations for the future. If you haven't noticed, I've kind of taken a liking to you.

Caleb: Do you give all the people you like black eyes?

Me: Oh my god. How many times do I have to apologize? I was asleep when I elbowed you!

Caleb: "Asleep"

Caleb: I'll tell you one of these days, Zoe.

Me: Thank you. <3

Caleb: Did you just less than three me?

Me: Shut up.

Me: What do you think about these throw pillows?

Me: DOWNLOAD ATTACHMENT

Caleb: I try very hard not to think about throw pillows at all.

Me: BE HELPFUL DAMMIT.

Me: Give me your opinion.

Caleb: Funny. Last time I tried to give you my opinion, you told me how they're just like assholes.

Me: I'm sorry. I mean, I was right, but I'm saying sorry now because I want your help.

Caleb: I like your honesty.

Me: Great. So, what do you think about the pillows?

Caleb: They're fine.

Me: Fine as in "they look good" or fine as in "ew no"? Because there are two very different things, you know.

Caleb: Oh, I know. I've lived with you long enough now to know the many, MANY different meanings certain words and phrases have.

Caleb: And they are fine as in they look good. Sky blue fits us.

Me: Back the truck up. What exactly do you mean by "many different meanings"? Elaborate.

Caleb: No, because you know exactly what I'm talking about, and I know if I "elaborate" I'm somehow incriminating myself, allowing this conversation to be used against me in the future.

Me: Oh wow. Is THAT how you think of me? That I'll just hold on to one tiny conversation for ages and ages and then BAM! Bring it up when you least expect it and throw it in your face?

Caleb: Yes.

Me: Smart man.

Caleb: SEE!

Me: HEY! I was kidding. Mostly.

Caleb: MOSTLY she says.

Me: So, sky blue then?

Caleb: Sky blue is fine with me.

Me: Like FINE fine or...?

Me: ;-)

Caleb: Goddammit, Zoe.

Caleb: Well, it's done. I officially sold my bike.

Me: YOU WHAT!

Me: Why?

Caleb: I have to pay for physical therapy and these fucking medical bills somehow.

Caleb: Bike had to go. I got a pretty penny, so it'll help.

Me: And what are you going to do for transportation now?

Caleb: Bus. Walk. Exchange kisses for rides.

Me: Well hell. That really sucks. I'm sorry you had to get rid of it.

Me: But I hope you're only exchanging those kisses with me…

Caleb: We'll see.

Me: Uh huh. I'll remember that tonight when you try to kiss me or get fresh with me.

Caleb: Is that what the kids are calling it these days? Getting fresh?

Me: It's what I call it. Like father, like daughter. Get over it.

Caleb: I think you were born in the wrong decade. You should have been born in the mid 80s so you could have grown up as a true 90s child. That would have been a good decade for you. You and your weirdness and those fucking denim coveralls you wear when you paint would fit in just fine.

Me: DON'T YOU DARE MAKE FUCK OF MY DENIM!

Caleb: Make fuck of?

Me: FUN OF.

Me: You knew what I meant, you ass.

Caleb: Sometimes with you it can be quite the guessing game.

Me: Are you saying I'm difficult? *cracks knuckles*

Caleb: Yes, but in, like, a good way.

Me: That's what I thought. Kisses! Gotta run!

Caleb: She threatens me and then runs off. Da fuck.

Me: You love it.

Caleb: I thought you were leaving?

Me: I would if you'd shut up already!

Caleb: So sassy today.

Me: SHHH!

Caleb: Fine, fine. I'm being quiet now.

Me: Doesn't seem like it to me.

Caleb: Stop answering me then!

Me: Never. I love having the last word.

Caleb: You don't say.

Me: I do.

Me: ;-)

Me: Hey Caleb…

Caleb: What do you want?

Me: How'd you know I wanted something?

Caleb: Your tone suggested it.

Me: Ah, yes, I forgot all about that superpower of yours.

Caleb: Well, spill it.

Me: Can you do me a solid and pick up a pizza on the way home?

Caleb: Pizza? You want PIZZA?!

Me: Pleeeeeeease? *bats lashes*

Caleb: Sigh. Fine. We can have pizza.

Me: YES! Double cheese and pepperoni and green peppers.

Caleb: Ham and pineapple or no deal.

Me: You're going to make me barf.

Caleb: Then no deal.

Me: Caleb...

Caleb: FINE. Just this once.

Me: You're the best.

Caleb: BUT, I'm going to knock on the door and pretend I'm the pizza man. You have to answer in your sexiest pair of pajamas. Deal?

Me: Deal.

A KNOCK SOUNDS at the door and I grin.

Game on, Caleb.

"Who is it?" I say in the huskiest voice I can manage.

Caleb chokes out a laugh. "Pizza boy, ma'am!"

I wait five seconds before swinging open the apartment door.

"My, a special delivery just for me?"

His mouth drops open. "*That's* your sexiest pair of pajamas?"

"Yep."

"Well played, Zoe." He shakes his head, amused. "Well played."

I do a curtsy and grab the pizza he's holding. "Thank you."

He did the say the sexiest pair of pajamas, not the pair

I look sexiest in. Wearing jammies with a topless Captain America on them is technically me wearing my sexiest set.

"I'm going to need to watch my words with you, huh?"

"It wouldn't hurt." I stand on my tiptoes and place a quick peck on his lips before grabbing his shirt and pulling him inside.

There's a flash of surprise on his face, which is understandable since this is one of the first times I've initiated a kiss between us, but he quickly brushes it off and closes the door behind him, trailing behind me as I make my way to the kitchen counter.

I drop the pizza and open a cabinet, pulling down two plates before grabbing two bottles of water from the fridge. I set everything down in the front of where Caleb's seated.

"Dig in."

We each grab two pieces and stuff our mouths full of gooey cheese and pepperoni.

"So," Caleb starts, "I talked with my manager about that little Outer Banks trip we discussed the other day."

"And?"

"He's cool with me taking the time off. They had only planned to schedule me for one day while we plan to be gone and one of the other women who works there just happens to need a few extra hours."

"Does this mean we're going?"

"If you promise me that meeting your parents isn't going to be an awkward nightmare, then yes."

"I make no promises." I clap my hands together and

squeal. "Eep! I am so excited! This is going to be so much fun!"

"What are we going to do besides each other?" He waggles his brows up and down. "Kidding. But really."

"First, no bangin'. Second, we can shop or get facials or—"

"I have a feeling your version of a facial isn't my version of a facial."

I wink his way. "Guess we'll find out, huh?"

"Zoe!"

"What! You started it!"

"Yeah, but I was kidding."

I feign surprise. "Oh, uh, yeah, me too." He nearly chokes on his pizza. "Kidding, kidding! You're the one being pervy. I didn't know you were so dirty, Caleb."

"I'm not. Well, maybe a little, but not like creepy pervy."

"Well that's good to hear. No one likes creepy pervy."

I take another bite of my pizza and think about how I want to approach what I need to tell Caleb next.

"So..."

"Yes?"

"I, um, I went to visit Delia the other day."

He grabs for another slice of pizza. "Cool. How'd that go?"

"It was good. We talked."

"About what?"

I don't say anything, instead grabbing for my water and downing nearly half the bottle.

"Zoe," he presses after several moments of silence.

"We talked about you."

"About me?"

I nod. "And my blossoming, um...feelings for you."

His eyes sparkle with amused mischief as he runs a hand across the stubble on his face, pretending to be perplexed. "You have feelings for me, huh? And here I thought you just wanted me for my good looks. I wasn't aware it ran deeper."

"You know damn well it's about more than your looks, Caleb."

He grins. "I was hoping so."

I turn my head, not wanting him to see the blush creeping up my face, but he seeks me out, reaching for my chin and pulling my attention back to him. His midnight blue eyes flick between my hazel ones and my lips.

"Because it runs deeper for me, Zoe—a lot deeper."

I swallow the lump in my throat and dart my tongue out to wet my dry lips. "Good."

He closes the distance between us, stretching over the counter to press a soft, sweet kiss to my waiting lips.

That's all it is, one small kiss, and then he's settling back into his seat, bringing his slice of pizza back to his mouth.

So why does it feel like so much more?

Mittens jumps onto the counter, somewhere he's not usually allowed, and begins to rub against me.

"What about him?" Caleb asks. "Is he going with us?"

"Oh definitely. There's no way I'd leave the little guy here."

"And your parents are cool with bringing him?"

"Are you kidding? My mom is half in love with him already and she hates cats, and my dad cannot wait to snuggle the little guy."

Caleb tilts his head at me. "Have you been sending your parents pictures of my cat?"

"Hell yeah I have. He's adorable as shit!"

"You're not wrong." He dips his head down. "You also know he's sniffing at your pizza, right?"

I glance down. "Shit! Mittens!" I shoo him off the counter. "Get!"

He takes off, his paws slipping against the counter, causing his legs to catch my plate and flip it up. My pizza goes flying into the air and makes a loud smack against the kitchen floor.

I look down at it, annoyed. "Guess I should just be glad it's not on the carpet."

Caleb smiles at me sheepishly. "Sorry. He's really cute though."

"Argh. I know."

I pick up the slice of pizza and deposit it in the trash before pulling off a paper towel and wiping up the mess on the floor.

"So, uh, what did Delia say?" Caleb asks.

I peek his way and notice how he's not looking mine. He's curious, but he's also scared. He doesn't want her to hate us either.

I rest against the counter, staring at him. "She wants me to be happy."

"And are you?" He finally looks at me. "Are you happy, Zoe?"

"I'm well on my way there."

CHAPTER 16

"WE NEED to head to bed. We're going to have a long day tomorrow."

We.

The word rolls off his tongue so easily, and I love the way it sounds.

Caleb and I have been sharing a bed for a few weeks now and, much to my surprise, it's been tame. We've spent several nights kissing until our lips are numb, but it's not moved any further than that.

He clicks off the TV and stands, holding his hand out to me. "Come on."

I place my hand in his and let him pull me up. "But I'm not sleepy."

"If you at least come lie down, I'll make sure to wear you out."

He sends me a saucy wink, and I barely hold in my laugh as we make our way down the hall to my bedroom.

Our nighttime routine is habit now. Caleb pees then brushes his teeth while I slip off my bra. Then I brush my teeth while he changes into his sleep pants, moves all the pillows off the bed, and folds the covers down.

Coming back into the bedroom from the bathroom, I click off the light just as Caleb's pulling the blanket up and around his neck.

"Ugh. Am I going to have to fight you for the covers all night long again?"

"Maybe...but you secretly like it."

"How could I possibly like it?" I say, climbing into bed and nestling down next to him.

"Because then I'm all warm and cozy and you get to snuggle up close to me."

"Is that what you think? That I *like* sleeping plastered to your side so your boner pokes me in the back all night long?"

"Yes."

I laugh at his honesty. "You're only half right."

"That's good enough for me." Caleb stretches an arm around me and pulls me closer to him. "Hi," he says on an exhalation.

"Hi."

He presses a feather-light kiss against my forehead and I sigh.

"Did you just sigh?"

I stiffen at his question, self-conscious. "No."

His body shakes with laughter. "Liar."

"You are so annoying."

"But you like me."

"That's highly debate—"

Caleb's lips capture my own, and suddenly we're lost in a kiss.

The way he moves his mouth over mine, the way his soft lips feel, it's all so...noteworthy, and I can't seem to get enough of him. I want more—*so* much more.

We roll until he's lying on top of me, our lips never once disconnecting. I'm pressed against all his good parts as his mouth continues to work mine over, his tongue pushing against the seam of my lips. I open for him and nearly sigh again as he invades my mouth.

His movements are so slow, calculated. It's like he's making love to my mouth. His hips are rolling into me just as his tongue sweeps over mine. He knows exactly what he's doing to me.

He pulls his mouth from mine, running his lips down my chin and over my throat before blazing a path down to my chest. His hands snake under the t-shirt I'm wearing, slowly climbing higher and higher until I can feel his fingers graze the undersides of my breasts.

We've never gone this far before. He knows, and I know it too.

His eyes find mine, seeking permission, and I nod.

Gently, he cups my breasts, and he's delightfully surprised when he finds what's waiting for him.

"Your nipples are pierced?"

"They are."

He drops his head into the crook of my neck, groaning.

"Oh fuck, Zoe." He rocks his hips against me again. "Fuu-uuuuck. You're killing me here."

"Caleb."

He doesn't move, but I can feel his heavy breath on me as he tries to calm himself.

"Caleb," I say again.

This time he lifts his head, and his dark blue eyes are nearly black.

"Pull my shirt off."

Moments later I'm lying topless, hair fanned out around me, a hungry Caleb staring down at me with pure desire.

"Can I…"

"*Please*," I beg.

He holds my stare as he dips his head and closes his mouth around my left nipple. I nearly fly off the bed. The perfect pressure, the perfect connection…

He's the perfect guy.

I wrap my legs around his waist, pulling him closer with every touch. I hold his head to me as his tongue sweeps over my nipples, taking time to kiss and suck on each one. His hips drive into me, his erection rubbing against my clit with every move he makes.

My panties are soaked, and I know he can feel the evidence of what he's doing to me.

"Caleb…" His name leaves my lips on a moan.

"I know, Zoe. I know."

He reaches down between us, his hand dipping into

the waistband of my sleep shorts. His fingers graze over my mound, sliding down until he finds my clit. He begins drawing slow, lazy circles with the tips of his fingers, and I want to scream and cry and fall apart all at once.

Between his mouth on my breasts and his fingers on my clit, I'm about to combust.

"I...can't... It's too much."

My nipple pops free of his mouth, his teeth catching just the tip, and it's enough to send me over the edge.

My legs begin to shake, back arching off the bed. I can't seem to catch my breath as my orgasm washes over me.

I can feel Caleb's smile against my cheek as he peppers kisses across my face.

"You okay?" he asks.

"Oh yeah."

He laughs and rolls off me, sitting up next to me. "Good."

"Are you okay?"

"Me? Oh I'm good."

"Do you need me to...you know."

He flashes his eyes downward. "You did."

"What?" I lift up on my elbows and peer around him.

Sure enough, there's a wet spot on the front of his shorts.

"Did you come in your pants without me even touching your dick?"

He coughs out a laugh. "When you put it that way, I

sound like a juvenile teenager who can't control his pecker."

"No, no, it's not that. It's actually kind of...hot."

"Hot?"

"Oh yeah. A woman loves when a man loves pleasuring her. That's proof right there that you got off on me getting off."

"Or it was me basically grinding into your mattress."

I shake my head and lie back down against my pillow. "Don't ruin the magic, Caleb."

He leans over, his arms caging me into a box as he stares down at me.

"That was all you, Zoe. Watching you fall apart, feeling you beneath me..." His eyes dart to my exposed breasts, gaze turning lustful again as he bites at his lip. "Those fucking nipple rings of yours..." His attention returns to me. "It was all you."

I grab at his shirt and pull him down until I'm able to press a kiss against his lips. "Good."

He points to his lap. "I'm going to clean this up. Sleep."

"We would have been asleep ages ago if you weren't all over me."

"It's your fault you're so irresistible."

"That so? I'm going to hold you to that, Caleb."

He mutters something indecipherable as he makes his way to the bathroom. I hear the shower kick on and I roll over onto my side, thinking.

First, I can't get over how intense that orgasm was. I felt everything at once. I could feel each flick against my nipple, each stroke against my clit. Even more than that, I could *feel* Caleb, and not in just the obvious sense. I could feel his emotion, his need. I was so tuned in to him, I wasn't sure where he began and I ended.

I've never had that before, never been so in sync with someone.

It felt...good. So fucking good.

I'm surprised we went as far as we did tonight, surprised at the gentleness and care he demonstrated, and his reaction to my nipple piercings? *Ugh.* His eyes were so lit with fire and hunger and desire. I can't remember the last time a guy looked at me with that much want.

Caleb's turning into something so much more than I thought he would.

My silly moments of *damn he's hot* have become a sense of deep desire. I crave his presence, can't wait for the next moment he puts his hands on my body and sets it ablaze.

"You still awake?"

I nearly jump at the sound of his voice. I was so lost in thought that I didn't hear the shower turn off or him creep back into the room.

He climbs into bed and settles down against me, wrapping his arm around me from behind and pulling me close. He places a soft kiss against my exposed shoulder and I sigh.

"You sighed again."

"I did."

I can feel him smile.

"Hey, Caleb?"

"Yeah?"

"I like you...a lot."

"I like you a lot too."

"Let's not screw this up, okay?"

He's quiet for several moments before he finally says, "I'll do my best, Zoe."

CALEB HAS one hand resting on my thigh, one holding the steering wheel as we blaze our way down the highway to Outer Banks. Mittens rests on the floorboard between my feet, soaking up the afternoon sun. The windows are down, and the cool breeze is blowing through my loose hair. My road trip partner is wearing his signature ball cap, this time turned the right way, the edges of his blond hair peeking out beneath it.

I think a few days of freedom are going to do us good. After last night, this trip feels like the start of something more between us, and I think I'm ready for it.

Reaching over, I run my fingers through his hair as it blows loose, enjoying how the soft curls feel. "I kind of dig your hair longer like this."

"Yeah? I always hated my curls."

"They're sexy on you, plays into the boy-next-door thing you have going on."

He grins. "You know, I'm not as innocent as you'd like to think, Zoe."

My cheeks heat. "After last night, I'm starting to believe that."

"So, did you grow up in Outer Banks?"

"Nope. Northern Virginia. My parents moved down here when I left for college."

"Why Outer Banks?"

"Why not? Beach *all* year long—what's not to love about that?"

He lifts his shoulder. "I'm not a big beach person."

"Really? I figured you'd be all for it."

"Nah. I mean, it's not bad, but I'm not going to go out of my way to get there, you know?"

"That kind of makes me sad. I love the beach. Soaking up the sun, listening to the waves crash against the shore—it's one of my happy places. I was so thrilled when my parents decided to move to OBX."

"Maybe you'll convince me to love it like you do."

"I hope so. I'd hate for that to be the deciding factor in whether or not I want to date you."

"And do you, Zoe? Want to date me?"

"I think I do."

"Think? Or do? Come on, sweet girl."

I take a deep breath, not answering for several miles.

Do I like Caleb? Yes. Do I want to date him, turn this kissing roommates thing into something more? Yes. Am I scared as shit? Hell yes.

But I think I'm ready to let go, to let myself find that happiness Delia keeps talking about, and I think I'm ready to find it with Caleb.

"Do."

I can see the grin that overtakes his face in my peripheral.

"Told you you wanted me."

I glare over at him. "Shut up."

"It's okay. I want you too."

"That was made evident last night."

"Speaking of last night...your nipples—when did you get those?"

"Not too long ago, maybe six months." I place my hand on his leg, running my fingers in circles, moving closer and closer to his dick. "You're the first to see them."

Caleb coughs and shifts in his seat. "I am, huh?"

"Yep."

"That, uh, is something I like."

"Yeah?" I say, my fingers inching closer and closer to his growing erection.

"I'm driving, Zoe."

"So?"

"Get your hand away from my dick."

"Or..."

"Or two can play this game."

"You could always pull the car over," I suggest.

"Not gonna happen. We have a schedule and I'm sticking to it. Besides, do you want to explain to your parents why we're late to meet them? I don't want their first impression of me to be that I can't be on time."

I pull my hand away at the mention of my parents, crossing my arms and pretending to pout. "Fine. You win."

"That's what I thought."

Another few miles pass before I ask, "So, do *you* want to? Date, I mean."

"I'm down if you're down."

"I'm going to tell them you're my boyfriend then."

His head snaps my way. "Wait, who? *What?*"

Laughing, I gently push his attention back to the road. "Watch where you're going. I'm going to tell my parents you're my boyfriend."

"I am?"

"We agreed we want to date, right? So I guess that makes you my boyfriend." I pause. "And I let you touch my lady bits and see my nipples—that *totally* makes you my boyfriend."

He shakes his head, amused. "I guess it does."

"So it's settled, right?"

"It's settled."

Something hits me, and I lean forward in my seat a bit, the anticipation of hearing the answer to my next question too much to contain. "And we're...exclusive?"

"I don't know about you, but I've been exclusive this whole time."

"Good." I sit back. "That's good."

"Zoe?"

"Yeah?"

"I'm real glad you're my girlfriend now."

"Me too, Caleb. Me too."

CHAPTER 17

"NERVOUS?"

"A little." Caleb pulls his cap off his head and stuffs it into a pocket on the duffle bag he's holding. "I've never met a girlfriend's parents before."

"I like it when you say that."

"What? Girlfriend?" I nod. "Me too."

"But you've never met the parents before?"

"To be fair, I started this trip as your kissing roommate and you roped me into being your boyfriend on the car ride. I wasn't prepared."

I let out an unattractive snort. "You act like I forced this girlfriend-boyfriend thing on you. It's not a big deal."

He meets my eyes, his stare serious. "Yes, it is."

There's a sincerity and seriousness in his voice that makes me realize that maybe all these feelings I've been rapidly developing aren't one-sided, and maybe Caleb's feeling them just the same as I am.

My heart begins beating so hard and loud, I fear he's able to hear it.

"Am I wrong, Zoe? Is this just a fling to you?"

I shake my head. "No."

He studies me, trying to read all the emotions running through me—excitement, fear, nervousness, happiness.

"Good."

"Good," I echo.

I lift my hand, ready to press the doorbell. "Last chance to run."

He shakes with laughter. "Press the damn button, Zoe."

We hear the bell chime throughout the house, and we wait.

And wait...and wait.

No one ever comes.

"Are you sure this is the right house?" Caleb asks.

I glare at him. "I know where my parents live."

He tucks his lips in, eyebrow shooting up. "Whatever you say."

I pull my phone from the purse I have dangling from my shoulder and swipe until I find the video chat option. Hitting the green button next to my mom's face, I hold the phone out and wait for her to answer.

My mother's face—or should I say, her *nostril*—fills the screen.

"Mom, move the phone away from your face."

She complies and gives me a wide grin. "Ah! There's my beautiful girl!"

"Here I am, but where are you? I thought you and Dad would be here until tomorrow."

"Well, we were going to, dear, but your dad—" She shoves her phone into his face. "Say hi, Rafe."

"Hi Rafe," my dad deadpans.

My mom's face comes back into view. "He never wants to play along. Anyway, he decided to whisk me off for a romantic stay at a B&B before we go visit your grandmother."

"I'm only doing this to get a decent meal!" my dad insists, and I believe every word.

For some reason, my grandmother will *only* eat dinner at a local diner...and the food is horrendous. I can't fault him for leaving early.

"Well, hell, I guess you're meeting my new boyfriend via FaceTime." I move until Caleb's in the picture. "Mom, Dad, this is Caleb, my boyfriend."

"Boyfriend?" my mom asks, surprised. "You told me he was just your roommate. When did this happen?"

Caleb and I exchange a glance.

"On the way here," I tell her. "We just decided."

She purses her lips. "Zohanna Marie, are you playing some sort of trick on me?"

"No, Mama. No trick. We're dating."

"Oh!" Her face lights up. "Well in that case, well done—he's a looker!" She sends Caleb a wink. "Hi Caleb, I'm Sofia. Sorry we can't be there to greet you, but we'll be back before the end of your stay. You'll have to give me lots of hugs then."

"Mama, I am standing right here. Stop flirting."

"And I'm sitting right here. Leave the poor boy alone," my dad tells her.

"Oh hush, Rafe. You know you're my number one this week."

The screen blurs and you can tell the phone's gone flying through the air, and then it's dark.

"Ah hell! Hang on, kids. I dropped the dang phone."

"Don't take your seatbelt off. I'm driving!"

"I will be just fine for two seconds. Take a chill pill, bro."

My mouth drops open. "Mama, did you just call Dad 'bro'?"

Her face comes back into view, this time with my dad in the background. "Well if he wasn't such a douchebag sometimes—"

"Mama!"

"She's been calling me that a lot lately, read some novel about these 'douchebag' wrestlers—"

"Hands *on* the wheel!"

"—and now she won't stop," he continues. "Also, hi Caleb. I'm Rafe, the better half of this duo."

"It's nice to meet you, Better Half Rafe."

My dad grins. "I feel like I should ask you something normal, like what's your major? Isn't that what dads are supposed to ask boyfriends, Sofia?"

"Sure."

"I'm majoring in sports nutrition, sir. I'm vying for a position with the team at the university and am hoping to get on board with them then eventually work my way up to a head coaching position."

"I'd say you're doing well with sports nutrition."

"Sofia! Leave the kid alone!" my dad admonishes.

"I'm just saying, looks like he's in *great* shape."

I stand there with my jaw slack, completely mortified by my mother's behavior.

"Thank you, Sofia," Caleb says with a smirk.

"PEACHES!" my dad shouts.

"RAFE!"

And the call goes black.

I stare at the screen, confused as hell.

"Peaches?" Caleb enquires.

"Yeah, not sure what that's about. Let's try to find the key though. There was a break-in up the road not too long ago and they've changed the locks since I was here last."

We look under the mat, inside the potted plant sitting next to the door, in the ones hanging on the porch...nothing.

"What about a barbeque pit?" Caleb suggests.

"Good thinking. Let's go around back."

I lead Caleb around the back of the house and hear him whistle when it comes into view.

"Holy hell. This is *nice*, Zoe."

"Isn't it? My dad takes a lot of pride in it. He's a contractor, designed and built this whole thing himself."

There's an extravagant circle deck coming off the back of the house with a built-in fire pit in the center and a fancy schmancy patio couch and chair surrounding it. A large stainless steel barbeque pit sits off to the side with a stone wall encasing it.

Just then my phone rings—another FaceTime call from Mom.

"Oh my gosh, your father is a mess!" she says once her face fills the screen. "He about ran us off the road trying to get to the roadside peach stand."

She holds the phone out and there's Dad, holding up a big bag of peaches with a cheeky grin on his face. "It's official—I'm movin' to the country. Got me some peaches to eat!"

"Is your entire family into 90s music?" Caleb says, knowing my dad is referring to the ever-popular *Peaches* by The Presidents of the United States of America.

"Guilty as charged, dear," my mom answers. "Is she still listening to that rap music?"

"She is, ma'am."

My mom shakes her head. "We tried to stick to the alternative and grunge, but she just couldn't give it up."

"I like a good beat," I say matter-of-factly.

"Whatever you say, dear. We're going to get off here. Just wanted to tell you we love you and sorry we couldn't be there to greet you. We'll be back before you leave though."

"It was great meeting you, Rafe and Sofia."

"See ya later, Caleb!"

My mom holds up her hand and gives us a peace sign. "Mama outtie!"

"Wait! Wait! Where's the new key?" I manage through a giggle. My mother has obviously gone insane.

"We slid one inside the fire pit out back."

"And Magnus?"

"He's locked in our bedroom, so be sure to let him out soon. He probably has to potty by now."

"I'll make sure to let him out ASAP," I assure her.

"And, Zoe, for the love of all things holy, please stay away from the kitchen. I do not want to get a phone call from the fire department again." Caleb falls into a fit of laughter. "See, I can tell he knows just what I'm talking about."

"Oh, I do," he tells her.

I swat at him. "Both of you stop! Go enjoy your night away. Love you guys!"

"Love you too. Great meeting you, Caleb! Enjoy the beach."

I disconnect the call and peek over at Caleb. "Well, those are my parents."

"They seem fun."

"Oh, they're something." I grab my bag that's been lying by my feet and haul it up onto my shoulder.

I walk over to the fire pit and laugh when I see the key sitting in plain sight, not at all hidden from potential burglars.

"They could have at least thrown a few logs in there or something," I comment.

I push the key into the lock and twist. I'm met by the sound of Magnus going crazy inside my parents' bedroom.

"Want me to go grab him?" Caleb asks.

"Sure. It's just straight down the hallway. I'll hold on to Mittens for safety."

Caleb hands over his cage and I let him out, wrapping him tightly in my arms as Caleb navigates his way to the bedroom.

About ten seconds later, my parents' sixty-pound boxer comes barreling out of the bedroom, jumping and licking at me. Mittens lets out a loud hiss and tries to scurry up my body farther, hoping to escape him.

"His leash is hanging right there." I point to the wall beside the back door. "Just run him out while I get Wolverine over here settled down."

"On it."

Caleb manages to get the leash on Magnus and out the door they go. I grab the cat bed and hustle Mittens back to the bedroom we'll be sharing, only letting him loose when the door is closed. He immediately curls into himself, staring at the door with wide eyes and perked-up ears.

"Just watch, you two will be best buds by the time this is over."

I leave the door cracked and walk back into the living room, where Caleb's just taking the leash off Magnus. The moment he's free, he darts down the hallway, and I can hear him and Mittens getting acquainted with one another.

"That's going to be fun," Caleb says as he hangs the leash back up.

"Oh loads. I was hoping my parents would be here to at least introduce them, but that's up to us now. He's better behaved when they're around."

I take a seat on the luxurious couch my mom bought last year and glance around the room.

The walls are a different color, specifically the accent wall behind the television stand. It used to be a pale blue but is now a darker gray, which fits nicely with the gray flooring they put in a few years ago. My mom has also swapped out her usual blue accent pieces for pale yellow ones, making the whole room brighter.

Caleb takes a seat next to me. "This is a beautiful home."

"Isn't it? It's perfect for the two of them too. I love coming to visit. They make it feel so homey."

"I'm sure anywhere your parents are feels homey."

"Is that the case for you too?"

"No. No it's not.

His focus is anywhere but on me, but I hear the sadness laced in his words.

I don't know if I want to kiss him, hug him, or cry.

"MY PARENTS LIKE YOU, you know. My mom texted me earlier with the stamp of approval."

Caleb lets out a relieved sigh. "Good. I was worried they'd hate me for moving in with their daughter and then, you know, not keeping things very roommate-like."

"Nah. They're pretty easygoing."

"They seem great."

We're sitting out back on the patio, stuffed from the Chinese food we ordered and curled up together in the chaise lounge, sharing a beer while a fire roars in the fire pit.

My dad's hung twinkle lights around the perimeter since I was here last, and they cast a romantic glow around us.

I close my eyes and rest against Caleb's chest, soaking in the sound of the waves crashing against the nearby shore.

"I love it out here."

Caleb kisses at my neck, his lips cold and wet from the beer. "Yeah, it's not too bad."

I smile, because I know he's referring to spending time with me just as much as he is our surroundings.

"Your dad kind of got me thinking...what are you doing after graduation, *Zohanna*?"

"You caught that, huh?"

"Hell yes I did. You never told me that was your full name."

"It's a little strange..."

"Strange?" I feel his lips at my ear. "It's sexy as hell."

I let out a shiver and can feel his laughter against me.

"Now, after graduation," he says.

"I..." My lips go dry. This is the first time I've had anyone other than my parents ask me directly. Even with Delia, it was always just a *we'll see when I get there* sort of answer. "I, um, I've actually applied for a few graphic artists positions, some freelance, some in New York—even one at a comic book publisher."

Caleb sits up behind me and I turn to look at him.

"Yeah?" His eyes light up. "That's amazing, Zoe."

"Thanks." I duck my head, surprised by how much I love his enthusiasm and encouragement. "Now, is what you were talking to my dad about what you really want to do?"

"It is. Well, *now* it is. With baseball gone, it's kind of my only option."

"And will you be happy doing that?"

He stares off into the distance, a look of longing on his face, and I know he's thinking about the career he could have had. Finally, he peeks over at me again.

"I will."

I regard him with searching eyes, trying to see if he's lying.

He's not.

"Good," I tell him. "That's good. And what about the...obligations you have here? Your mom and dad?"

Caleb lets out a sad laugh. "My dad isn't in the picture, Zoe."

"He's not?"

"No, it's just me, my mom, and my brother. That's the way it's always been."

"That's..." I take a shuddered breath. "Wow. I'm sorry to hear that."

"It's just life."

"I never knew that about you. You realize you never tell me anything about your family or past, right? That's the first time you've even talked about your brother before. I didn't know you had one."

"Is it really?"

I nod. "I think the only things you've told me are you're a huge comic nerd because you could get them for cheap, you lived in a trailer park, and as I've just discovered tonight, you don't know your father and you have a brother. That's it."

He scratches the stubble covering his cheek. "Oh."

"Yeah. *Oh.*"

We don't say anything else and eventually I return to my position, resting against him again. We listen to the sounds of the sea, the noise nearly lulling me to sleep, then Caleb finally speaks.

"I'm sorry, Zoe. I'm not trying to hide anything from you, it's just not something I like talking about. I prefer to keep that life separate from my life here. I don't want to blur the lines."

"That sounds nice in theory, Caleb, but your lines were crossed long ago. Being gone every Sunday, sometimes not coming back until the next day, rushing to take phone calls in the middle of the night..."

"You've heard those?"

"Sort of."

I heard the one when we fell asleep on the couch that one night, and then there have been a few times I've noticed him responding to texts at ungodly hours of the night.

"Shit. I'm sorry, Zoe."

"It's fine. I just want you to know that if this thing is going to work between us as more than roommates, meaning our newly minted boyfriend-girlfriend status, you're going to have to talk about it sometime."

He exhales a shaky breath. I can feel his heartbeat against my back, a sure sign he's nervous to open up.

"I suppose that's fair, but not this week, okay? Let's just enjoy this time together. Trust me, you don't want to hear about it now."

I twist around until I can look him in the eyes. "But I will when we get back?"

"When we get back. I promise."

CHAPTER 18

"ZOE."

A kiss to my cheek interrupts my peaceful sleep.

"Zoe."

Another peck.

"*Zoeeeeee.*" This time my name is whispered sweetly into my ear.

I peek one eye open and look at the digital clock resting on the bedside table.

6:30 AM. What in the hell...

"This better not be a booty call or I'm going to punch you right in the taint."

"It's too early to be threatening people with taint punches, Zoe."

"That is highly debatable." I roll over to find Caleb peering down at me, a goofy grin gracing his lips. "Why are you smiley and why are you waking me up so early? We're supposed to be on vacation. People *sleep in* on vacation."

"Not when their adorable boyfriend wants to watch the sunrise on the beach."

I eye him, wary of his intentions. "*You* want to go to the beach?"

"I want to go to the beach."

"Are you drunk?" I reach out and touch is forehead. "Do you have a fever?"

"No and no. I want to see this beautiful sunrise everyone keeps going on and on about."

"You want to watch the sunrise?"

"Are you just going to lie there repeating everything I say, or are you going to come with me?"

"Coming!"

"Oh, you will be later."

I groan and roll back over, facing away from him. "It's too early for your innuendos, Caleb."

"If it's not too early for taint punches, it's not too early for innuendos. Fair is fair. Now, up." He smacks my ass and flies off the bed, out of my reach. "We have a sunrise to catch."

"That was my ass, you ass!"

"I know, baby." He winks. "I was aiming for it."

He trots out of the room, mighty proud of himself, as I reluctantly climb out of the warm comfort of my bed.

I search through the bag I didn't bother unpacking last night, looking for something to wear. It's early morning and the wind on the beach is going to be chilly, so it's best I dress warm.

We spent last night wrapped together until well after

midnight, kissing and whispering in the dark. I'm thankful for the time we spent together, but less than six hours of sleep isn't enough.

He's lucky I like him.

I haphazardly pull on sweats and a hoodie then slide my feet into flip-flops, snagging my toiletries bag on the way out the door and across the hall.

I pop into the bathroom and run a brush through my hair before tossing it up into a messy bun. Then I brush my teeth and wipe the sleep out of my eyes before meeting an impatient Caleb out in the hallway.

"Ready?"

"I suppose, though you owe me coffee *and* breakfast after this," I tell him as I grab blankets from the linen closet he's standing beside.

"Is anything open this early?"

"Oh yes. You think you're the only one who wants to watch the sun rise?"

I lead us outside and across the street.

The road is quiet, most people still in bed at this hour as we walk about half a mile in silence until we reach the nearest beach access point.

We amble our way down the well-worn pathway and Caleb reaches out, grabbing my hand as we walk onto the beach together.

"It's chilly out here."

"Yeah, I should have warned you," I say. "Good thing I

grabbed an extra blanket though. We can sit on one and wrap up in the other."

"You're too good to me."

Caleb stares out at the ocean in awe as we approach the shoreline. His ball cap is resting backward on his head, eyes still a little puffy from sleep. He threw on a plain black t-shirt and jeans, and was smart enough to wear sandals so the sand doesn't drown his shoes.

I watch as he takes a whiff of the fresh sea air, his nostrils flaring and eyes falling shut.

"Mmm, salt and fish," he says on the exhalation.

I pull at his arm, dragging him farther down the beach. "Oh, hush it. It's not that bad."

"Nah, it's not. I actually kind of like it."

"I see the ocean is already working its magic on you."

"Something like that," he mutters, now looking over at me.

"Stop being cheesy," I say with a grin. "Pick a spot for us to sit. We don't have much longer."

Caleb leads us to a spot several feet from the lapping waves before stopping and grabbing the blankets from my hands. He spreads out the smaller of the two and then sits, patting the space between his legs.

"Come on, let's be all romantic and shit."

"You can't say things like 'and shit' and expect to still come off as romantic," I chide as I cozy into the spot between his legs.

"It got you down here, didn't it?"

"The promise of a warm blanket got me down here. Nice try though."

Caleb wraps his arms around me as I settle into his embrace, his lips finding my neck in no time. He nuzzles against me and I sigh, resting back into him more.

The sun begins its ascension over the horizon, setting the purple haze of the clouds on fire with orange and yellow rays of light. The sight is beautiful, and I'm reminded how no sunrise is ever like the last, the colors always playing off one another differently.

I've sat on this very beach watching the sun come up so many times, but somehow, sitting here with Caleb for the first time, it feels different. The colors of the sky are a little brighter, the air crisper, the waves more bold and beautiful.

It feels new and fresh, just like how *we* feel, and it was worth waking up for, that's for certain.

"This was a good idea," I say aloud.

"Just think, you hated me not fifteen minutes ago."

"Hate is a strong word. Let's just say I wasn't your biggest fan."

"And now?"

"You're okay, or at least you will be when you buy me breakfast."

He nuzzles my neck again, the contact sending a chill through me. "Thank you for coming out here with me. I've never seen anything like this before. It's breathtaking."

"Told you there was nothing like it. I'm glad you cajoled me out of bed to see it."

"Cajoled, huh?"

"That's fancy talk for coaxed."

He laughs, his mouth vibrating against my skin. "I know what cajoled means, Zoe."

"Hey, just checking. I know I don't brain well when I haven't had my coffee."

"Are you saying you want to get breakfast now?"

I push off the ground in a rush and grab at the blanket he has wrapped around him. "I mean, if you're offering…"

He takes the hint and stands, shaking the sand off the other blanket as best he can then folding it.

"Back to the house then?"

"Oh no. We're going to That Pancake Joint. It's only about half a mile up the road."

"You sure you don't want to go back and change first?"

I glance down at what I'm wearing. "Why? You embarrassed to be seen with me?"

"Not at all."

"Uh huh. So what you're saying is I'm looking buttass ugly right now and need to go change."

"What? No!"

"But you think *I* think I look that way?"

He shakes his head back and forth, eyes wide. "I'm so confused right now, and a little scared of saying anything."

Laughing, I pat his shoulder as I walk by. "Shit, Caleb.

I'm giving you shit. Come on, we don't want to hit the breakfast rush."

"ROSCO! MY MAN!"

I high-five the guy standing behind the counter at That Pancake Joint.

"Zoe! How the hell ya been?"

"Pretty good. Been busy as hell with school, but you know how that goes. You almost finished with your degree?"

He smiles broadly. "I graduate at the end of the summer."

"Nice!"

"When you bringing that pretty friend of yours back here? I miss her."

"And I told you last time, you old snake, she's taken now."

"Watch it, kid. I'm not *that* old." He nods toward Caleb. "Who's the pretty boy? Your next victim?"

"She kidnapped me, sir. I was wandering the beach, just trying to find my way home, and she stole me away, demanding I buy her breakfast."

Rosco grins. "Yeah, that sounds like her."

"Rosco, this my new boyfriend Caleb. Be nice to him."

"Yes, ma'am." The guys shake hands. "Nice to meet

you, and I'm really sorry you're caught up with the likes of her."

"Thanks. I appreciate that."

"Asses," I mutter. "Can we get a table for two, please?"

"Like you have to ask," Rosco says. "Go grab your table. I'll be over in a minute."

I lead Caleb over to my favorite spot, a booth in the back that faces the ocean.

"I take it you've been here a few times?" he asks as we slide into the bench seats.

"Every time I visit, multiple times. It's my second favorite place here."

"The first being the beach, right?"

"Bingo bango."

"Is that how you met Rosco?"

"Nah." I grab the sugar holder and pull out three packets before pushing it back to its spot. "I met him on the beach. He was out there selling these horrid t-shirts that said, *I got crabs in Outer Banks*. On the back, *From your mom*. I had to buy the guy a slice of pie after that."

"Oh shit." Caleb chokes back a laugh. "I don't know if that's ballsy or just really stupid."

"A little of both, I think. Anyway, next time I came in, he was working here. I've stopped by to see him every time since."

"That's kind of awesome. And he's in school?"

"Yep. Just finishing up his bachelor's degree. He's a really great guy, but don't tell him I said that."

"Too late. He heard ya." Rosco slides up to the end of the table. "What'll you two have? Your usual, Zoe?"

"Please? Get that for Caleb too. I know he'll like it."

"You got it." He taps the table twice. "I'll be back with your coffees."

"What'd you order me?" Caleb asks when Rosco leaves.

"You'll see."

"It better not be anything weird."

"I never eat anything weird."

"Not true," he argues. "I once rinsed out a bowl that had three different kinds of cereal *and* orange juice in it."

"Hey, don't knock it till you try it."

"Is she on about the orange juice and cereal again?" Rosco says, setting two cups of steaming hot coffee on the table.

"It's not *that* weird," I tell them.

Rosco makes a disgusted face at Caleb and points my way. "Please tell me you notice something's wrong with her."

"Oh definitely."

"Asses!" I say loudly, nearly yelling.

Rosco walks away cackling, and Caleb dodges the sugar packet I throw his way.

"I think I might like it here," Caleb comments.

"Because you have someone else to back you up and join in while you pick on me?"

"Pfft, obviously." He takes a sip of his coffee. "That, and everyone seems so...jovial, so free."

"You've met like one person other than my parents."

"Hey, those people on the beach waved at seven in the morning."

"That's a fair point."

"But really, it's not bad so far. I'm not hating it, so that's a plus."

"You thought you'd hate it?" I ask, surprised.

"Not like *hate* it, more like I wasn't sure. Outer Banks is a nice place. You always hear about people vacationing or retiring here. It's the 'it' place, you know?" He folds his hands around his mug, staring down into the dark liquid. "I come from the opposite side of the tracks, like *way* far away from any of this. I'm always afraid people can tell I'm a huge fake."

I peel open the sugar packets and dump all three into my coffee before adding a heavy dose of creamer, taking in what Caleb just said.

This isn't the first time he's mentioned coming from an unsavory neighborhood, so that part doesn't surprise me.

What does is that he's so down on himself for where he came from, like that's his fault.

Does he not see how far he's risen above it? How much better he's made his life in just four years away from there? Sure, he's still attached to it in some way, but that's not him anymore. That place isn't who he is. He got out. He's making a better life for himself.

Can't he see that?

"I don't think you're a fake, Caleb. Where you're from? That's not *you*. Your dreams, your goals, those aspirations you hold so dear to your heart? *Those* are you. The rest of it only defines you as much as you let it."

He finally looks up from his coffee, meeting my eyes. "Is that how you see me? Full of dreams and goals?"

"I see you in so many different ways. I see those sad, unsure parts of you. I know there's a string tethering you to your old life that you can't seem to break, but I also see the dreamer, the boy next door. I see the third baseman, the nice guy, the amazing friend and supportive shoulder to lean on." I pause and lick my lips, hoping what I want to say next doesn't offend him. "Can I tell you something?"

"Of course."

"When I first met you, I had you pegged for the average meathead jock. Then you started dating Delia and I knew that couldn't be true because that was so not her type. So, I just moved you into the nice guy category, and I won't lie, you stayed firmly planted there for some time. Then when everything went down last year with the photo and you were right there on the battlefield with us, I started to see other sides of you." I brush a stray hair out of my face and tuck it behind my ear, blowing out a breath. "That's, uh, when you piqued my interest...popped up on my radar, so to speak. You were kind and fierce and loyal and so...*there*, you know? You dropped everything. You raced to the rescue, and not just because you felt you had to, because you wanted to. You stepped up and got dirty when you needed to. I really respected and admired that."

He doesn't say anything, just stares at me.

I take a sip of my coffee and clear my throat. "You're not so one-dimensional, Caleb, and you kind of rock my world because of it."

Caleb shifts in his seat, not meeting my eyes. I can tell he's feeling a bit uncomfortable with everything I just admitted, but it feels good to get it off my chest.

I watch him stare out the window, his brows drawn tightly together, mouth crumpled in the corners in concentration.

Just as I'm about to say something to change the subject, he opens his mouth.

"You know, that's when I really started noticing you too. I mean, you were always this kind of force to be reckoned with, but it wasn't until Delia went through all that shit and you were there for her that I realized how great you really were." He finally looks my way. "Do you remember that night you went out with Delia after she and I broke up?"

I cover my face with my hands. "I was *so drunk* that night."

He peels my hands away and gives me a lopsided smirk. "I meant before that part. You were just so...free, and fun. I was there for a while before I finally approached you two, just sitting in the corner watching you dance and flirt your way around the room, hoping and praying you'd come flirt with me too." He winces. "Then I felt like such an ass because Delia and I had just broken up."

"I kept calling you a douchebag the entire night and you wanted me to flirt with you?"

"I said before you were drunk, remember?" he teases. "Anyway, that was the first time I really felt a pull toward you. It's increased every time I've seen you since."

My heart is pounding in my chest at his words, my ears starting to thrum to the beat.

"Every time?"

"Every damn time. Hell, even though I live with you, it still increases daily. There's just something pulling me closer and closer your way." He shakes his head. "God, I sound so stupid."

"I feel that too, Caleb." I turn my attention to the window, my head swimming with so many thoughts. "According to Delia, it's a good thing. She says we're falling," I say almost absentmindedly.

Just then Rosco appears at the end of the table, plates in hand.

"All right, two stacks of peanut butter banana pancakes, extra whipped cream, and a sprinkle of chocolate chips. Plus a side of bacon," he says as he deposits our meals.

"Oh god, it looks just as good as I remember," I nearly moan.

"Tastes just as good too," Rosco promises. "You guys need anything else?"

"Syrup?"

He holds up a finger. "Ah ah." Reaching into his apron, he pulls out a bottle of syrup that I know for a fact is going to be warmed and sets it on the table. "For the lady."

I give him a thumbs-up. "We're good to go then."

He throws me a wink. "I'll be back for my tip in a bit. Enjoy."

I grab the syrup and pour a hefty amount all over my plate, including on the bacon.

"This is either going to give me a boner or a sugar rush," Caleb says as he begins cutting into his pancakes. "Or both."

I watch as he takes his first bite, his mouth closing slowly over the fork before he pulls it out clean. His eyes float closed and his body slacks in ecstasy. I would know, because I've been that person before.

"Fuuuuuck. You've ruined me, Zoe. Completely ruined me."

"It's amazing, isn't it? You're welcome."

"It's official: we're retiring here."

We're.

I don't miss it.

I'm certain he doesn't mean it in the way that's making my heart jump into my throat, but damn does the word feel good to hear.

We devour our meals in near silence, the only sounds are Caleb's moans and our forks scraping against the plates.

As we're pushing our empty dishes aside, Caleb speaks.

"For what it's worth, Zoe, you rock my world too."

CHAPTER 19

"THIS WAS ALL an elaborate plan to get me to dog sit with you, wasn't it?"

"No," I say not so innocently.

"Uh huh." Caleb rubs Magnus's ears. "She's a big fat liar, isn't she Magnus?" He barks. "See, even he doesn't believe you."

"You're full of shit, aren't you, Magnus?" He barks again, and I lift my brow, silently saying, *See, he's clueless.*

"Mittens is not thrilled with this situation right now."

He's not wrong. The cat is currently curled into a ball on my lap, throwing daggers his owner's way. Mittens is rather displeased by Magnus's constant need for attention from Caleb, and he's even less happy that he's now resting his head in his lap and staring over at him with mirth.

"I'm sorry, buddy. I'll make it up to you." Caleb goes to pet Mittens, but he bats away his attempt.

"Oooooh, sick burn, Mittens! High five." I grab his paw and bump it against mine.

"You're both horrible."

"Says the betrayer."

Caleb throws his arms in the air and Magnus whines at the loss of his touch. "It's not my fault he's attached to me." He covers the dog's ears. "The craziest part is that I don't even really like dogs."

As if he can hear and understand him, Magnus chooses that moment to amble away, head dropped low.

"Great, now you've hurt his feelings, Caleb."

"He'll be all right." He turns toward me. "So, plans for tonight?"

"Can't we just sit on the couch like we've been doing all day? It's so comfy here."

"I can't deny that, but nope. I want to take you out. It'll be our first official date as boyfriend and girlfriend."

"That's not true—we went to That Pancake Joint."

"Okay, how about our first *romantic* date, huh?"

We've been at my parents' house for several days now, splitting our time between soaking up the beach rays, hiking, and being lazy on the couch. To say it's been relaxing is an understatement, but I can't deny that I'm getting a little bored. Maybe a night out will do us some good.

I groan. "I guess I can put pants on for one night."

Caleb grabs at the blanket I have covering my lap, trying to peek underneath. "You didn't put any pants on after the beach? I want to see."

I swat away his attempts. "Get out of here, you pervert! You cannot talk dirty to me when I have a kitten in my lap. That is just weird, Caleb."

He lifts Mittens from my lap and holds the cat out in front of him, mock glaring at him. "You're killing my game, bro."

Mittens responds by licking his paw and not giving two shits. Caleb lets him go and then turns my way, his eyes darkening with desire.

He moves onto his knees and crawls toward me across the couch, his lips pulled into a teasing smirk. "Now, about that no pants thing."

He's lying on top of me now, settled comfortably between my legs.

"What?" I say.

"Are you really not wearing pants?"

"Maybe."

He rolls his hips into me and I do everything I can not to gasp at the contact, but he can tell. He can feel it, can see the reaction in my eyes.

"Maybe...yes?"

"Maybe."

Another roll into me. "Any answer yet?"

"Nope."

"We're going to be here all night at this point." He titters.

I lift a shoulder. "Or I'm just waiting until you get me off."

He lets out a surprised half-gasp, half-laugh kind of thing. "You're such a little shit."

Then he's kissing me. His tongue begs for entrance

and I allow it, pulling him closer and wrapping my legs around his waist, my heels digging into his ass. His lips move over mine with such finesse that it's not long before *my* hips are the ones rolling. I'm desperate for any sort of contact. I grab at his shirt and he pulls away long enough to rip it off over his head, somehow still keeping that stupidly sexy baseball cap on his head.

Goddamn.

I race my hands over the muscles of his back, digging my nails in with just enough bite to keep it fun.

He lets out a gasp, the sound lost in the moans I emit as his erection drives into me again, rubbing against my clit. This feels reminiscent of our past activities, but somehow the need for more is stronger, harsher.

I want Caleb naked, and I want him naked now.

I drag my hands down his back and straight under the band of the boxer briefs he's wearing beneath his sweats. I stop for only a moment to admire the number of squats he must do for his ass to feel this good before I trace a light path around to his front. I take my time teasing him, gently running my fingertips over his thighs before finally palming his hard cock.

Caleb tears his mouth away and rests his forehead against mine, his severe breaths so loud in the otherwise quiet room.

"We have to stop," he begs as he pushes his hips into my hand.

He wants this just as much as I do, maybe even more.

"Why? We've been playing this game for days now. You keep dancing me to the edge and then BAM! You back off. I don't even have balls and my balls are blue. You kiss me, touch me, and you won't leave my stupid nipple rings alone, but you won't bang me?"

"What? I like the antici—"

"Say it!"

He frowns. "I was going to before you interrupted me."

"Never mind," I mutter. "You'll learn one day. Now, explain yourself."

"If you think I don't want to sleep with you, you're wrong. I'd fuck you right here on this couch, but I don't want that for our first time together. I want the moment to be right." He pulls his head back and meets my eyes. "We're getting dressed. We're going out to dinner. Then we're coming home and I'm having *you* for dessert."

My hand tightens around his length at his declaration, my teeth biting into my bottom lip at the promise.

"Zoe?"

"Yeah?"

"Move your hand before we can't stop."

He's right. I know he is. I don't want our first time to be on the couch either.

But I want him—*bad.*

With reluctance, I remove my hand, and Caleb pushes

himself up on his knees and away from me. I sit up, my hair spilling out in every direction, chest pushed out, on display.

His pupils dilate as he points to the bedroom. "Go now, before I change my mind."

Chuckling, I pull myself off the couch, keeping the blanket wrapped around my waist because I am most definitely *not* wearing pants under it. "Where are we headed?"

Caleb relaxes back into the cushions, exhaling a shaky breath and widening his legs, trying to make the situation in his pants more comfortable. "Seafood okay?"

"*Is seafood okay*, he says to the girl who spends several weeks a year in Outer Banks."

"That's Zoe speak for yes, right?"

"Yes, Caleb."

He runs a hand over his forehead, pretending to wipe sweat away. "Phew. Good."

"Give me about thirty minutes then?"

"Like thirty minutes or 'thirty minutes'?"

"A normal half hour."

"Okay," he agrees skeptically.

An idea hits me as I begin to walk away, and I pause at the end of the hallway.

"Hey Caleb?"

He twists around on the couch to look at me, the fire of desire still dancing in his dark eyes. "Yeah?"

I drop the blanket, and his mouth hits the floor along with it.

"A thong!" he yells. Then I hear a loud groan as I continue down the hallway. "You're killing me, Zoe. Killing me!"

CALEB SHIFTS the car into park and opens his door.

"Stay there," he instructs over my shoulder.

"You could at least say please!" I argue, but he's already shutting the door.

I watch as he rounds the car and am surprised when he rushes over to my side to open my door for me.

Extending his hand, he says, "For you."

I allow him to help me out while eyeing him warily. "Why are you being so gentlemanly? Because you want to get laid? I plan on sleeping with you either way."

He smiles. "No, but that's nice to know."

"Then..."

"It's the right thing to do. When we were at the restaurant, I watched an older man do it for his wife and I realized how much of an ass I was for never doing it before."

I want to laugh at him, but it's actually kind of sweet and romantic.

"Well, thank you then."

"No problem."

He grabs my hand and begins leading us down the path we always take to the beach.

I pull at him. "Wrong way."

"No it's not."

"You're telling me *you're* dragging *me* to the beach for a change?"

"What? I'm starting to like it."

I grin. "Hey, I'm not arguing here."

We make our way down the dusk-lit path. Before we hit the sand, we take our shoes off and Caleb rolls up the bottoms of his jeans. Then he leads me over to what we've sort of deemed our spot and doesn't stop until we're standing at the water's edge.

He wraps his arms around me from behind, pulling me close, and we stare out at the vast ocean as the rays of day settle into night, letting the water lap at our bare feet. The stars shine above, the moon reflecting off the water in a picturesque scene. It's quiet and comfortable and the simplest, most romantic gesture of my life.

"I could get used to this," he says into the darkness. "You, me, nights on the beach."

My heart thunders at the thought of spending days, weeks, even years with Caleb out here.

"Going out to romantic seaside dinners...roasting s'mores on the beach."

I can see it too.

"Spending all the time in the world out here...naked. Lots of naked time on the beach."

A laugh bursts out of me and I spin around in his arms. "You totally just ruined that moment. Also, being naked on the beach does *not* sound appealing. Sand would get in all your no-no spots, and no one likes that."

"What the hell are you doing? Lying spread eagle face down in the sand or some shit? We'd lay a blanket down. Geez."

I pat his chest twice and walk farther into the water. "I love how you're planning our beach sexcapades right now. Never gonna happen."

He prowls toward me. "You don't think so?'

"Nope."

"You're telling me if I stripped naked right now then slowly peeled away that"—he bites his knuckles and takes another step closer—"sexy as sin sundress from your body, you wouldn't get down and dirty with me?"

My chest heaves as the image of Caleb doing just that washes over me. I have to squeeze my thighs together to create even an ounce of the friction my body is craving right now.

"No," I lie.

"Uh huh." Another step. "And what if you were *all wet* and *had* to get naked? What about then?"

I already am wet. "No."

"You sure?"

"Yes."

Suddenly he swoops me into his arms, my legs automatically going around his waist for safety, and dashes into the shallow part of the sea. I'm half enthralled, half scared I'm going to fall.

He brings his lips to my ear. "I'll say it again: you sure?"

"I swear, if you drop me into this water, Caleb Mills, you're going back to school with the bluest balls in the history of blue balls, and you're going down with me."

He gives me a wide grin then pretends to lose his grip on me, and I let out a loud yelp, climbing farther up his body.

"Caleb!"

"Zoe!"

"Put me down."

"Down? Right here?"

I rear back and glare at him. "Don't you dare."

Laughing, he carries me until we're not standing in half a foot of water and are safe on the beach again. When we're in the clear, he releases his strong grip.

I slide down his body in the slowest moment of my entire life.

I feel him everywhere, every hard and soft inch of him. I feel his heart beating within his chest like a wild animal stuck in a cage.

His opaque blue eyes bore into me, and we're locked in a trance. Our chests brush together at every strangled breath, and I know he's feeling what I'm feeling.

I don't know if it's the magic of the moon or the anticipation building up to our date tonight, but I want Caleb.

I want him *bad*.

I lift my head until my lips meet his ear. "Caleb?"

I feel his shiver, can hear the shuddered breath he takes. "Y-Yeah?"

"Take me home."

WE WALK hand in hand up the short driveway, only parting to unlock the front door.

Caleb silently leads me down the hall to the bedroom we're sharing.

The backs of my knees hit the end of the bed and I collapse, bouncing once before finding my balance. He stands in front of me, looking down at me like I'm his last meal.

His hands come up to cup my face, titling my head until I'm at just the right angle, and then he descends. His lips move over mine with ease, his tongue slipping into my mouth. One hand stays cupped along my jaw while the other dances upward. I feel his fingers dive into the mass of hair I have swept up into a ponytail and carefully pull the elastic band from the mess.

He grips my head and holds me close to him as his mouth makes love to mine in the most sensual kiss I've ever experienced. My whole body is alight with fire and yearning. My body is growing lax with the pleasure coursing through me, and all he's doing is kissing me.

I can feel it everywhere—in my nipples, which are pulled tight and straining against the barbells poked through them, in the way my core tightens and my thighs clench together at the anticipation of satisfaction to come.

More. I want more.

I reach for the button on his pants, working it through the hole and popping it open. With an agonizing slowness, I slide the zipper down. I find the waistband of his jeans and push them and his boxer briefs down until his hard cock is exposed.

I waste no time wrapping my hand around his arousal.

Caleb wrenches his mouth from mine with a gasp.

"Zoe...what are you doing?"

"Shut up. Let me take care of you."

"T-Take care of me?"

I stand and maneuver us until Caleb's sitting on the bed and I'm standing over him, his dick still bobbing between us. I fall to my knees and push him back until he's more relaxed.

He grabs at my face, his hand cupping my jaw and bringing my eyes to meet his.

"You don't have to," he insists.

"I know I don't *have* to. I *want* to."

His cock jumps at my words and I chuckle before

lowering my mouth to him. I dart my tongue out, tracing it around the tip.

Just the tip.

I laugh to myself and Caleb moans at the vibration it sends over his dick. I trail my tongue down around his length, taking my time teasing him.

"Zoe..."

I finally close my mouth around him, sucking him all the way to the back of my throat before retreating and repeating the process.

Suddenly Caleb grabs my head and pulls me off him.

"No. No! You're fucking deep-throating me and that's just not fair. I'm about to bust a load down your throat, and that's not what I want to do."

I sit back on my haunches, giggling.

"You're laughing? Ugh. How come you never told me you could deep-throat?"

"What'd you want me to do? Introduce myself with that little factoid?"

"Hell yes!"

I titter. "That would take all the fun out of the surprise."

"I suppose that's true," he murmurs.

He pulls me to my feet along with him and grabs at the straps on my dress, slowly pulling them down.

"There's a zipper in the back, you know."

Caleb spins me around and pulls me tightly against him. I can feel his erection nestled perfectly against my ass as he carefully rocks his hips into me. His chest brushes against my back with each inhale he takes, the warmth of his breath fanning across my clammy skin, sending a shiver down my body.

He gingerly pulls the zipper down the tracks, and I swear he's taking his sweet ass time.

Without an ounce of patience left in me, I grab at my dress and begin to pull it over my head, only to have it get stuck halfway.

"Ugh! Stupid boobs!" I grumble, jerking left and right, trying to pull the piece of fabric off me.

Caleb's hands find my body and still my movements.

"Oh, no. You're not going anywhere. You're staying just like this."

"Caleb, my dress is halfway up my body and I'm stuck."

"Exactly," he mutters. He leads me to the bed, pushing me down until I'm bent over, my ass in the air. "I see you put another thong on." His fingers pinch at the material. "I never understood how women could stand wearing them, but fuck me if I'm not enjoying the view right now."

"Fucking you is exactly what I want to do," I practically growl.

"In good time," he promises.

He pushes my dress higher, the new position making it possible for me to slide it over my arms and off. Caleb allows it, his attention still focused on my behind.

I gasp when I feel his lips land along my spine and

nearly collapse when he tracks the tip of his tongue down, down, down. His wet mouth lays open kisses along my ass cheeks, hands gripping each one.

"You been doing your squats, Zoe?" he whispers.

"Oh my god, shut up and just fuck me."

He bites at me and I buck into him. "Not yet."

His kisses continue south, his fingers now pulling at the thin strip of material resting between my cheeks, each pull causing friction in the most delicious of places.

I wait with want as he pulls aside my underwear and kneels, his fingers edging closer and closer to my now exposed pussy. A loud moan escapes me when he brushes his fingertip over me. I push my hips back, seeking more contact, but Caleb uses his other hand to hold me still as he continues slowly running a single digit over my skin.

He presses down on the small of my back, pushing me farther into the bed. I'm on full display, and I've never been splayed out like this in front of a guy before. It's sending a thrill through me I never knew I was missing.

Normally I'd be covering myself, embarrassed by having a guy so close to my privates, but with Caleb, I feel free. I feel confident.

Wanted.

Just when I begin to think this was all one big tease, he plunges two fingers into me. A gasp bursts free and my hips instantly push back on his assault.

The pleasure reaches an all-time high when his tongue

joins the torture, seeking out my clit and pulling it into his mouth with a tender suck.

"Oh, *holy fuck*, Caleb."

My legs begin to quake, and I can barely hold myself up as my orgasm races through me before I even know it's happening.

His rhythmic movements cease as he pulls away, sliding his fingers slowly out of my greedy body. He gently pushes me over until I'm on my back staring up at him. Reaching down, he hooks his fingers into my underwear and pulls the material down my legs while I catch my breath.

Standing with a foil packet in his hand, his fire-filled gaze meets mine.

"Scoot up the bed, Zoe."

That rasp. His voice sends another shock straight to my core, and I don't hesitate to comply, scampering up until there's room for us both. He tears the condom open and rolls it over his length, giving his cock a few strokes. I could watch him do it all day, and he knows it by the way my legs drift open at the sight.

He places a knee on the bed and lifts a brow my way.

"You sure?"

I nod enthusiastically.

Caleb wastes no time settling between my legs and burying himself in me.

"*Oh god,*" he croaks.

Panting, he pulls out until the tip of his cock is sitting

inside of me. "Fuck. You feel so amazing. I'm going to embarrass the shit out of myself if I keep this up."

I wrap my legs around him, heels digging into his ass, trying to pull him back in. "I don't really care about any of that. I just want to feel you inside me."

"*I* care. I want this to last. I want this to be good for you."

I grab his face, holding his stare steady with mine. "If you fuck me fast now, you can fuck me longer later, again and again and again."

I pull his mouth to mine and kiss him until he finally drives into me again.

His hips piston in and out of me as he reaches down to run circles over my clit with the tips of his fingers. We find a rhythm that works for us both, grunting and groaning until we can't take it any longer.

"I can't last much longer."

"I know, I know. Harder."

My pussy clenches around Caleb's dick and he picks up his pace, driving into me faster and harder than before. The pressure feels so good, so intense. It's just the perfect amount of everything, causing another orgasm to rush through me.

Another hard pound, another sound of our skin smacking together. Another moan, and then Caleb's finding his own release, his dick pulsing inside me as he empties himself.

His arms begin to shake as he holds his weight off me,

grinning like he's the luckiest man alive. He brings his nose to mine, nuzzling against me with his eyes closed.

"*Zohanna*."

It's all he says.

My name, whispered.

And I fall so hard for him.

CHAPTER 20

I STRETCH my arms wide above my head, my body feeling tired and sore in all the right ways.

Burying my face into my pillow, I smile at the thought of last night because...*wow*.

After we cleaned ourselves up in the shower, we slipped beneath the sheets and stayed awake for hours, exploring one another.

I don't think I've ever had so much fun learning someone else's body before.

I reach over to the spot beside me, surprised when I feel cold sheets.

Huh.

I peel back the comforter that's wrapped around me and reluctantly crawl out of bed. Picking up one of Caleb's discarded shirts, I slide it over my head and sigh as his scent washes over me. I dig a pair of socks from the duffel bag I've yet to unpack and pull them onto my feet before padding out of the bedroom and down the hall.

I expected to find Caleb sitting on the couch, but he's not there.

Instead I find a forlorn looking Magnus, who looks up at me with the saddest eyes.

"What's up, buddy?"

He lets out a soft grunt.

Okay then.

I wander into the kitchen...no Caleb.

Maybe he's out back?

Nope, not there either.

Bathroom?

Nope.

Out front?

Nada.

Where the hell are you, Caleb?

I race to the bedroom for my phone and check for messages. I come up empty...again. I pull up my recently contacted list and swipe over his name.

The call goes straight to voicemail.

What the...

Soft fluff rubs against my legs and Mittens lets out a tiny *meow*.

"Not now, buddy," I tell him, but he doesn't go away. He continues rubbing and pawing at me until I finally bend down and scoop him into my arms.

I run my hand over his fur, trying to console him and me at the same time, until my hand brushes over something that shouldn't be there.

Glancing down, I'm surprised to see a folded orange note attached to the back of his collar. I pull it free and set

Mittens down.

My hands shake as I open the note.

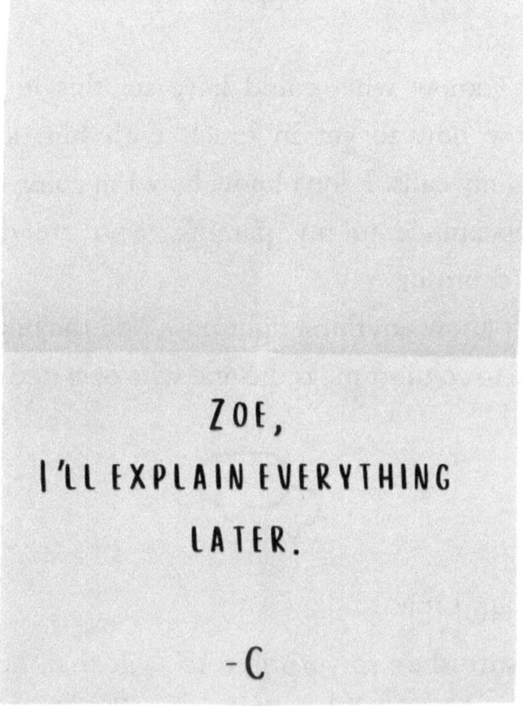

That's all it says.

Four words.

Four *fucking* words.

What in the actual fuck?

I try Caleb's number again. This time it rings twice before going to voicemail, which means he's deliberately avoiding me.

"Son of a bitch!"

I throw my phone onto the couch, annoyed as hell.

Did I do something wrong? Did we fall into bed too soon after declaring our relationship?

But seriously...what happened in the six whole hours of sleep I got?

I don't know what could have set this in motion. I don't know how to get in touch with him if he's not answering my calls. I don't know how I'm going to explain his disappearance to my parents, who are due home tomorrow morning.

I don't know anything right now, and the one person I want here to comfort me is the one who deserted me.

"WE'RE HOME!"

"I'm sure she's so surprised to hear that, honey. You did just text her to tell her we were pulling into the driveway," my dad says dryly.

Mittens goes flying off my lap at the invasion of new voices, skidding down the hall to the safety of his bed.

I climb off the couch with hesitancy, knowing my mother's reaction will be very dramatic when she sees me. My eyes are circled in dark bruises from lack of sleep and my hair is a hot mess. I wasn't able to sleep for more than an hour last night without Caleb's body pressed against mine.

I miss him.

I'm mad at him.

And I still haven't heard a single peep from him.

I go from being worried one moment to fuming the next. I just want to find a middle ground somewhere.

"Hey, did you—"

My mother's hand flies to her mouth just as I expected it would.

"Dear lord, Zohanna. What's happened? You look a mess."

Just as you rehearsed, Zoe. Play it cool.

"I'm not feeling well, Mama. Think I might be coming down with something. I'll probably head back home tonight."

She wraps me into her embrace and I sag into her, letting her comfort me for reasons she's unsure of. "Nonsense. You'll stay the night as planned. We'll feed you soup and send you back to school tomorrow."

I nod against her shoulder.

"You sure everything is fine? Where's this handsome-as-sin new beau of yours?" She lets out a girlish giggle that I can't help but smile at.

"He had to take off. His...old roommates were being troublesome about his bike he left over there."

Her brows pinch together, and I can see my father look our way from my peripheral.

Shit, did I tell them Caleb sold his bike? I can't remember...

They exchange a glance but don't say anything further.

"Well that's a shame. Did he at least leave his adorable little kitten behind? I was hoping to get a few snuggles in."

"He did. I'll go grab him."

"Wait, wait—no hug for your old man?"

I walk into my dad's open arms and he squeezes me extra tight, like he knows something's off. I blink back the tears forming. I love my parents and their unconditional support, but right now I just want to be alone. I need time to figure this out, to decide how I'm feeling.

As soon as my father releases me, I dart down the hallway, locking myself in the bedroom Caleb and I shared.

I'm just so...annoyed.

Why couldn't he have woken me up? Why couldn't he have left more than four words on a piece of paper? And why in the hell can't he answer his phone? Text me back? Anything!

Pulling my phone from my pocket, I check it for the millionth time.

Nothing.

Still.

I think it's the total silence that's pissing me off the most.

I want to send him some *very* angry texts right now, but I know that's not going to get us anywhere. I can't muster up the energy to be fake nice, so I don't say anything at all.

Scooping up Mittens, I march toward the door and pause. I inhale a deep breath and square my shoulders.

Fuck this.

I'm not letting his disappearance ruin my time with my parents. I'm going out there with a smile on my face and enjoying the rest of my break, Caleb Mills be damned!

CHAPTER 21

Caleb: I'll be home tomorrow.

Caleb: Sorry I had to leave. There was some shit I had to take care of.

Me: You know, Caleb, there's always "some shit" you have to take care of, and that's fine. I understand you have obligations and everything, but not leaving in the middle of the night RIGHT AFTER WE HAVE SEX FOR THE FIRST TIME would be a good idea.

Caleb: It wasn't YOU. It was me.

Me: CLICHÉ!

Caleb: But the truth!

Me: I'm sure it is. That still doesn't excuse you just leaving and then not even bothering to answer my calls the entire time you're gone. Not bothering to send a single text. Not bothering to give me ANY details as to where in the hell you disappeared to.

Me: I don't get it. We're dating, right? That's that WE decided. Boyfriends and girlfriends don't just ghost on each other. That's not how relationships and communication work.

Caleb: We talked about this though. We said we'd discuss my home life when we got back.

Me: We did, but that does not mean you can LEAVE IN THE MIDDLE OF THE NIGHT and then NOT TALK TO ME.

Caleb: I shouldn't have done that. I'm sorry.

Me: Apology accepted, but it doesn't change how pissed I am.

Me: Being left stings. Being left NAKED in bed stings even more.

Me: Not to mention you left me there to explain to my parents, who were very much looking forward to meeting you, where the hell you were.

Me: And your cat. Can't forget you just left him there too.

Caleb: It really wasn't you. I promise.

Caleb: And I'll be sure to apologize to your parents. That was a dick move.

Me: Yeah, you keep saying that, but it's not what it felt like.

Caleb: I'm sorry I did that to you. It wasn't fair.

Me: Again, I accept your apology, but I'm still angry.

Me: I think I still need some time to cool off. I have a project due next week and I need to focus on that. I think you need to take some time to decide how you're going to continue to juggle your life here and your life there, because these lines keep blurring and it's starting to suck.

Caleb: What does that mean for us?

Me: I'm not sure, Caleb.

Caleb: Are…are we breaking up?

Me: No, I don't think we are. I think we're just sort of…figuring things out.

Caleb: That scares me.

Me: I know. Me too.

Caleb: I'm sorry I left you. Sorry you had to deal with your parents alone. Sorry I missed out on the rest of our vacation.

Caleb: I feel like I'm stuck between two worlds with obligations I can't seem to walk away from in both.

Caleb: I am just so damn sorry.

IT'S NEARLY midnight when I hear the keys in the front door.

I've been lying in bed for nearly an hour now trying to sleep, a new issue for me with Caleb being gone. I've grown so used to having him here that I can't seem to get comfortable without him. I can feel every lump, every dip, every cold inch of the bed.

It upsets me too much to sleep.

I can hear him rustling around the apartment, hear his quiet murmurs directed to Mittens. I listen as he locks himself in the bathroom, the squeak of the shower knob turning resonating off the walls.

Half of me is itching to open the door and climb into the shower with him. The other half wants to stay right here.

That part wins.

He stands under the spray for a solid twenty minutes

before the water shuts off. I stifle a laugh when he lets out a string of cuss words after he realizes he went in there with no change of clothes.

The bathroom door is pulled open and I slam my eyes shut.

Caleb pads into the room and my heart beats so loud, there's no doubt in my mind he knows I'm awake.

Drawers slide open and closed, and though he's making a concerted effort to be quiet, everything sounds so loud in the darkness.

The bed dips beside me, and suddenly all the air in the room is sucked out.

I can't move.

Can't think.

Can't breathe.

Caleb slides his arm around me and places a kiss on my exposed shoulder. He buries his face into my neck and inhales.

I don't even flinch.

"*Zoe.*"

He utters my name likes it's a curse and a prayer.

I missed hearing it. I missed him saying it.

I missed *him*.

I fight with myself, wanting to roll over and embrace him, but also wanting to block all this out and just rest, deal with it in the morning.

Yeah, the morning sounds good.

For the first time in several nights, I fall into a peaceful slumber, and I have no doubt it's because Caleb's arms are wrapped tight around me.

Caleb: I wanted to let you know I won't be home until after eleven tonight, so I can't make dinner.

Me: I work tonight, so it's no biggie.

Caleb: Oh. I thought you had Tuesday off.

Me: I normally do, but we had someone quit and the slack needed to be picked up.

Caleb: Makes sense.

Caleb: I want you to know that I am NOT avoiding you. I've just been busy. I assume you know that, but I wanted it to be very clear.

Caleb: I miss the shit out of you and am thankful you haven't locked me out of your room yet.

Me: I couldn't do that. You're too cozy at night.

Caleb: Ha. Is that the only reason you keep me around?

Me: No.

Me: I care about you.

Me: I'm still peeved, but I care.

Caleb: I know, and I'm sorry. I'll explain everything more to you later, but I want to have that conversation face to face.

Me: When?

Me: Because I'm kind of dying over here, Caleb.

Caleb: When is your schedule clear next?

Me: Clear as in clear for me? Or clear as in coincides with yours?

Caleb: Shit. Good point. Probably with mine.

Me: I have all of Thursday off. No class, no anything.

Caleb: That will have to work then.

Caleb: Zoe?

Me: Yeah?

Caleb: Thank you for not hating me and for giving me a chance to explain. I miss you.

Me: I miss you too.

CHAPTER 22

"MISS? IS THIS SEAT TAKEN?"

I glance to the empty spot to my right and frown.

"No. It's all yours," I tell the stranger.

It *should* be taken, but it's not.

I woke up this morning to a cold, empty bed and a text from Caleb that just said, *We'll talk tonight.*

Then tonight came around and he never showed.

So, I left, because there's no way I'm missing my monthly Rocky Horror date to wait around on a guy who keeps ghosting on me and standing me up.

The last week's been reminiscent of when Caleb first moved in. We're on completely opposite schedules, never having the chance to stop for a real conversation. He's been busy making up the hours he missed while in Outer Banks, and I've been wrapping up my senior project.

If I'm being honest, I haven't once rushed home to see him. I'm still a little peeved at him for ditching me on vacation, leaving me naked and alone in bed, left to fend for myself with my parents.

Since no real conversations have happened between us since he slunk home in the middle of the night, I don't have any more information. I want some answers, and I don't think that's too much to ask for.

I'm mad, but I didn't lie when I told him I still care. I really do, and that's the hardest part of all of this—having *feelings*. It's why I've always stuck to flings. They're easy, no attachments. I don't need to add to the list of heartaches I've had in my life.

Of course, the one guy I decide to give things a real shot with has commitment issues of his own.

Fucking figures.

I want to go back to running from feelings and hiding from all this bullshit. It was easier than whatever the hell is happening now.

"Thank you," the guy says, squeezing into the seat beside me.

He begins digging around in the prop bucket provided by the theater, pulling out the instruction sheet and attempting to figure out what the hell it is he's supposed to do.

Virgin.

The lights dim, the famous lips flash onto the screen, and a spark of glee flits through me. It doesn't matter how many times I've seen this movie, I still get excited when the credits begin to roll.

Except for this time.

As much as I love Rocky Horror and look forward to this night every month, something feels so off about it. I'm supposed to be here with Caleb. Everything with us is supposed to be fixed by now, but he's gone, and nothing is patched back together.

The guy sitting beside me digs into his bucket again, trying to prepare for the audience's first course of action.

"Rice," I tell him.

"Huh?"

"You're looking for the rice. That's the first prop you'll need."

He sends a grateful glance my way. "Thank you so much. This is my first time."

"I know. I can tell."

"That obvious?"

"You'll get the hang of it. Just follow my lead."

Someone kicks at my seat and I turn around, glaring at whoever's sitting behind me. There's plenty of room between the chairs and no reason mine should be getting kicked.

The theater is dark, but there's no mistaking that he's dressed in a full-blown Dr. Frank-N-Furter costume.

I give him a cursory glance before turning back around and putting him out of my thoughts.

The first song comes to a close and then we're heading off to church to watch Brad Majors (Asshole!) and Janet Weiss get engaged.

The poor guy next to me is too nervous to really give his rice a good sling, so most of it ends up in the hood of the person sitting in front of us. He's really the highlight of my night as the movie continues rolling and I walk him through his prop bucket.

A third kick of the night connects with my seat, and I'm officially pissed.

What is this guy's deal?

I lean over to the stranger sitting next to me. "Is he kicking your seat too?"

He looks at me, eyes wide. "Who?"

Another kick.

"That jackass behind us," I say.

"No, I don't feel a thing."

"The hell..." I mutter. "Maybe I'm just imagining it."

I do my best to ignore his kicks the rest of the movie, noticing they only happen when I talk to the man next to me.

Ass.

The lights briefly flicker and the virgin damn near jumps out of his seat. This is probably my favorite part of the show.

"Chill. They're just requesting for everyone in costume to come down to the front for the burlesque number. It's much more fun with about twenty or more Franks and Rockys on stage."

"B-Burlesque?"

I chuckle at his innocence. "Every theater does it differently, and this is where ours brings the 'actors' up on stage."

He nods and focuses back in on the show.

I feel the guy behind me hit my seat as he gets up to strut his stuff in front of the packed audience, and I sneer in his direction.

He responds with an amused grin.

Dick!

I resist the urge to throw something at him and watch as he moseys his way up to the front. I don't understand at all how he's walking in those six-inch stilettos. I can barely handle a four-inch heel.

The "cast" gathers on the stage, and I find myself drawn to the asshole who's been sitting behind me the whole show. He stands tall above the rest, telling me he's at least six-foot without the heels. His eyes flick about, and I wonder for a moment if this is his first time.

Then suddenly his eyes are on me and he's grinning like a fool. Just before the music begins to play, he blows me a kiss.

Perplexed, I sink into my seat to avoid his stare.

"I'm going to assume that was meant for you," the guy beside me whispers.

I don't respond. I can't respond.

Because something is making itself abundantly clear to me.

That guy decked out in briefs, fishnet garters, a red corset, and a boa is none other than the man I've been swiftly falling in love with.

A huge grin overtakes my face, and he knows I'm onto him.

I watch with amusement as they dance through the entire *Rose Tint My World* scene. The whole thing is complete with the inevitable trip and loss of wig. There's not a dull moment throughout, especially with my eyes on Caleb and his eyes on me.

He's up there, for me.

When the final scene plays, we all stand to cheer. The Franks and Rockys and Magentas and Riff Raffs take their bow before the audience swarms their friends and loved ones.

I wave to a few moviegoers I've come to know over the years and patiently wait for Caleb to stagger his way over to me.

The crowd is dwindling down when he finally emerges from the side stage.

One of the show's organizers is with him, and I see the guy give him a big pat on the back. Their lips move but I can't make out what they're saying.

Finally, after what feels like ages, he walks my way.

My breath catches in my throat, my heart pounding away in my chest in anticipation.

"Hi," he whispers when he's standing about a foot away.

There's a bit of lipstick still smeared across his lips, and my hands itch to reach up and wipe it away.

"Hi."

"How'd you like the show?"

"When in the hell did you find the time to learn those wicked dance moves?"

He grins. "That's why I've been out so late this week—Rocky Horror practice."

"You've been avoiding coming home and talking with me for Rocky Horror?" He nods. "I can't even be mad at that."

"Good."

I point a finger his way. "That doesn't mean you're off the hook, you know."

He sighs and takes a seat in the chair next to me. "I know. I have a lot to tell you."

"Yeah you do."

"How about we go home, huh? I'll tell you everything over breakfast."

"Breakfast?"

He pulls his phone from his pocket. "It *is* two AM."

My stomach growls as I contemplate his offer, and if the smile on his face is any indication, he heard it. I tip my head to the side and twist my lips, thinking.

"Can we have beats with this breakfast idea of yours?"

"Like you even have to ask."

I UNLOCK the door to the apartment and let us in.

Mittens comes prancing out of the bedroom and jumps straight into Caleb's arms.

"He's missed you, you know."

He runs his nose through the cat's fur. "I've missed you too, buddy."

We settle into a flow in the kitchen, me setting up the music and Caleb gathering all the fixings to make biscuits and gravy.

As I'm passing him on my way to the fridge to grab a beer, he snakes an arm around my waist and pulls me close. He places a finger under my chin and brings my eyes to his. Brushing the loose hair off my face, he smiles at me.

"Can I kiss you?"

My knees grow weak at the request, and I answer by crushing my mouth to his for the first time in a week.

It's a soft, slow kiss, but it burns in all the right ways as his lips move over mine. He lifts me off the floor and sets me on the counter closest to us, tucking himself perfectly between my legs.

Our kiss turns more intense, the pressure of his mouth growing against mine, his hands finding their way into my hair and holding my head to his. He kisses me like this is the last kiss we'll ever share, like he's afraid to let me go, like he's scared.

He has nothing to be afraid of.

I trace my hands over his back and around to his front. The moment my fingers meet his warm skin, he wrenches away, tearing his mouth from mine as he pants and gasps for air.

"Fuck," he mutters. "I'm sorry. I didn't mean for it to turn into that."

"Caleb, it's okay." I pull at his shirt. "I want this. I want *you*."

"I want you too, but you deserve answers."

In my lustful haze, I forgot all about how mad I am at him.

"You're right. Walk away."

"Huh?"

"Walk away. Go sit at the counter or something. I'll chop the sausage."

He rears back. "You're going to do what to my dick?"

"*The* sausage, not *your* sausage." His brows pinch in confusion and I point to the stove. "For the Bs and Gs."

"Ooooh. Well that makes more sense."

"Yeah, so scram. I can't have you near me right now. I want a clear head when you explain yourself."

He bobs his head up and down. "Right. Okay. You're right."

He takes a seat at the bar and lets out another ragged breath before bringing his hands together. He rests his fingertips under his chin, and it almost looks like he's praying.

"My mom hasn't always been the best mom."

I hop off the counter and head toward the stove,

thinking giving him the illusion of privacy while talking will help.

"She's a stripper—whatever pays the bills, right—but as you can imagine, working in an environment like that doesn't bring the best people into her life, especially since the town I come from is full of nothing but crime and filth and hungry kids. She's so...stuck there, and she's dragging my brother down right along with her. It's a damn miracle I got out."

I chop at the sausage with the spatula, still not turning around. "But did you really, Caleb?"

"Huh?"

"Did you really get out? You've been so stuck between the two worlds that I don't think you've escaped as much as you think you have."

I hear his hands hit the countertop, not in an angry way, but more like he's defeated. "It's so hard...so much harder than you can imagine."

"What's so hard about it?"

"They call, all the fucking time. They want me there—they *need* me there. They've run out of groceries, run out of booze, run out of money and cigarettes and everything else. And me?" He lets out a sardonic laugh. "I've about run out of fucks to give."

This is the first time he's spoken so freely about his family and it pains me to hear his words, to hear how broken and defeated he sounds. There's an underlying tone of panic too, and I sense that Caleb feels like he has to be the safety net that keeps his family afloat, forgetting to live his own life in the meantime.

"I threw away my shot at the majors for them." His voice strains, and I nearly drop my spatula to run to him. "I fucking threw it all away."

"What happened?"

"My brother owed some deadbeat guy money. He came looking for it, tried roughing him up, and I wasn't having any of that. The kid's only sixteen. So, I took care of things."

"Took care of things?"

"With my fists."

"Oh," I say.

"It gets better." He pulls his lips back in disgust. "The cops were called, and my mom *and* brother said I provoked the fight."

I spin around at his words, stunned. "No."

"Yep."

"That's... I-I can't even find the proper words for how messed up that is."

Moments of silence pass by. The food sizzles on the hot stove, and I don't bother to turn my attention back to it.

"Why do you keep going back?"

"My grandma. She lives in the local nursing home." He slides his eyes my way. "She's who I go see every Sunday."

"I thought you went back for your mom and brother?"

"I go back to give them money or whatever it is they

want. I meet them at the bus stop because I refuse to go over to their trailer anymore."

Huh. Interesting...

"And this last time you rushed home?"

His eyes turn to fire in a flash. "My mom called me hysterical in the middle of the night, told me my grandma had fallen, so I rushed there." He shakes his head, annoyed with himself. "I should have known it was a bullshit call—my mom doesn't care what happens to my grandma."

"Bullshit call?"

"Grams was just fine." He grins. "Nothing can take that old broad down. She's tough as nails."

"Then what did your mom want?"

That fire turns to ice, and I can see him stiffen. "Money."

"After all that, she called you for *money?*"

"Of course she did. She didn't think she did anything wrong."

"She didn't think..." I let out an irritated growl. I can't even with this information right now. "Why'd you end up staying longer?"

"Legal stuff. I'm now my grandmother's sole benefi-ciary and her only emergency contact. Now I don't have to deal with my mom or brother anymore."

I fold my arms over my chest. "And why couldn't you have explained this to me before?"

He lets out a loud sigh and scrubs his hands over his face. "I'm embarrassed as all get out by my family. My mom would rather be loyal to a drug dealer than her own son. My brother would rather become a drug dealer than finish high school."

Caleb stares blankly right past me. Watching the tangled web of emotions running over his face is killing me right now. He looks so...desolate.

"I've tried. I've tried so fucking hard to make things better for them. Hell, I even offered to move them here and away from all that bullshit there, but they don't want it. They *like* the way they live. How am I supposed to explain that my family wants that over me? Over stability? It's sad and painful and so fucking stupid." He finally looks at me. "I didn't mean to scare you, and in hindsight, maybe leaving a note like that wasn't such a smart idea."

"In hindsight?" My voice pitches on the last syllable. "You think?"

He shrugs sheepishly. "I'm sorry, Zoe. I'm really sorry."

"What about now, Caleb? What happens now?"

He sits up straighter, his chest puffing out with determination. His eyes harden.

"I'm tired of being their bank, tired of them using me, and I am damn sick of missing out on time with you. I'm done straddling the line. I don't want their toxicity in my life anymore. I want you."

"Me?" It comes out a squeak.

Caleb pushes himself off the stool and prowls toward me. His walk is strong, sure, steady.

He cups my face in his hands, tilting my head so I can meet his gaze. He towers over me with serious eyes.

"You, and this apartment. Breakfast and Beats. Mittens. Our grocery trips, the shitty schedules, and the texting. You. I want *you*."

"Are you sure?"

"I've never been more certain of anything in my life."

"Good answer."

He grins. "I know, huh?"

Caleb presses a quick kiss to my lips and I pull at his shirt, not letting him move.

I make sure he's looking into my eyes before I speak. "You have nothing to be embarrassed about, you got that? I'm here *for* you, not to pass judgment *on* you. We're a team. Don't you ever—and I mean *ever*—leave me like that again. Understood?"

He swallows loudly. "I got it."

I don't let him go.

"You know I'm not asking you to give your family up, right? That's not what I meant about you being between two worlds. It wasn't me giving you an ultimatum. I'm worried for *you*, for them, and kind of worried about us and what that could mean for our future."

"I like it when you say words like *our future*."

"Caleb..."

"I know," he says, pressing his forehead to mine. "But I *have* to. If I don't put my foot down and do something about it now, I won't ever do anything about it and I'll keep adjusting *my* life to meet their needs. I can't and won't do that. I'm getting ready to graduate college. I have a future to think about. I can't keep letting them drag me back to my past. I'm doing this for me, for us, and for them."

"You're a good man, Caleb." I push at his chest. "Now make me food. I'm famished and you're on my shit list."

"What?"

"Oh yeah, you're still in trouble."

"I am?"

"Yep." I nod. "But you'll be able to make up for it with lots and lots of nights spent in bed...or on the couch. The kitchen floor, the shower, the table..."

"But we don't have a table."

I shrug. "The counter works too."

"Are you trying to have sex with me, Zoe?"

"Not right now. Right now, you're going to finish making me breakfast."

"I thought *you* were the breakfast queen."

"Yeah, but it's part of your punishment."

He squints at me, not trusting my words. "Okay..."

"Great!" I clap my hands together. "Now strip."

"Excuse me?"

"Did you fart?"

He falls into a fit of laughter. "I'm going to regret teaching you that, I just know it."

I snap my fingers. "I don't see any stripping."

"Are you being serious?"

"As a fucking heart attack." I sweep past him and down the hallway. "I'll be taking my breakfast in bed!"

I hear the click of the burner being turned off and grin.

"Oh, me too," he promises as his footsteps thunder behind me. "Me too."

Me: DID YOU SERIOUSLY GHOST ON ME AGAIN?

Me: AFTER SEX?

Me: AGAIN?!?!

Caleb: Yes.

Me: And, pray tell, what is so damn important this time?

Me: Huh?

Me: CALEB! You have two minutes to answer me and then I'm getting up and leaving this bed and and...

Caleb: And what?

Caleb: Nothing? Yeah, that's what I thought.

Caleb: Now hush.

Me: Caleb!

Caleb: SILENCE!

I FUME, but don't text him back.

It's not even thirty seconds later when I hear the door open. I listen as Caleb moves around the living room, setting his keys on the table. I hear something land on the counter in the kitchen and then the rustling of a bag.

What the...

Then the familiar *thump thump thump* of bass blasts through the speakers in the living room.

A grin overtakes my face as the sounds of DMX filter through the apartment.

"There's the beats..." I mutter.

"I am walking down the hallway!" Caleb shouts. "I am entering the bedroom!"

I laugh at the smartass announcements and am pleasantly surprised when he walks in holding a box of hot, fresh Duck Donuts.

He crawls onto the bed, moving until he's resting against the pillows and headboard next to me.

"And there's the breakfast," I say.

"There's the breakfast."

I glare up at him, crossing my arms over my chest, just now realizing I'm only wearing a very thin white shirt. "I thought you had left me again. I woke up in a panic."

He sets the box of donuts on the bedside table and

turns to me. He pulls at my arms until he uncrosses them then leans in close. His hands cup my cheeks and he tilts my face, bringing my eyes to his, making sure I'm paying attention and soaking up every word he's saying.

"I told you, I'm done running back to them. I'm here now. They don't have any hold over me anymore. I want this life, with you. I want to be here, to be your boyfriend, your roommate. Just...yours, here, now."

"Here now," I echo on a whisper. "With breakfast."

"And beats," he insists.

"And beats. You're something else, Caleb."

"And you like it."

I lean into him, my lips hovering over his. "I do. I really, really do."

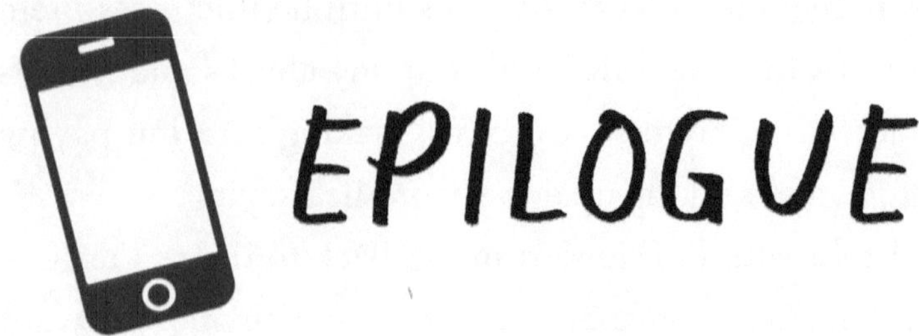

EPILOGUE

Ten months later

"EXPLAIN to me again why I'm doing this?"

"Because I'm cute and you adore me."

"Fuck," he mutters. "It's cold as shit out here."

"Shit is hot."

"What was that?"

I turn around. "I said shit is hot, like me."

"Did you just liken yourself to shit?"

"Oh." My mouth drops open. "Well, whatever. You know what I mean!"

He chuckles. "I d-d-do."

"Oh my gosh, stop being a big baby. It's not that bad out here."

"Says the girl who's completely bundled up right now."

"You have a coat on too."

"A coat, Zoe! A coat! I am wearing nothing but a pair of gold fucking booty shorts under this oh-so-warm coat of mine."

I grin. "And who's fault is that?"

He lets out a string of curse words. "Mine. I should have lied, should have said it was the worst damn meal I'd ever had in my entire life."

"You can't lie to the ones you love."

"I'm really starting to question just how much I love you."

"Because it's so much more than you imagined, right?"

"Sure, we'll go with that." He shivers again. "Seriously, are these doors opening soon or not? My dick is about to fall off."

"Quit being so dramatic."

To be fair, we *are* standing outside in about thirty-five-degree weather and Caleb *is* only wearing a jacket over his "booty shorts", but that's what happens when you bet your girlfriend she can't cook you a decent meal and she wins said bet.

"I cannot believe you made me dress up as Rocky."

"Should have asked the terms of the bet before agreeing and shaking on it."

"Seriously, you are so fucking lucky you're cute, and can deep-throat."

I smack at his chest. "Caleb!"

"What!"

"You are such an *ass*!"

"But you love it."

"So! Wait, I mean no!"

He waggles his finger at me. "Ah, ah, ah, I heard that. No take-backs."

"You keep this up and I'm divorcing you."

"We're not even married yet."

I lift a brow at him. "Yet, huh?"

"You're going to hold me to that, aren't you?"

"Probably."

He brings his lips to my ear. "I'm going to marry the shit out of you one day, Zoe. Just wait."

"Can you guys please stop? This is absolutely disgusting to watch."

"Yeah. I'm on the verge of vomiting, and I'm so ugly when I vomit."

"Everyone is ugly when they vomit, Zach," I tell him.

"Whatever. Just tone it down a notch, huh?" He turns to Delia. "How come you don't deep-throat me?"

Caleb and I burst into laughter as Delia starts smacking at him. "You are such an—"

"Ass! Say ass, Delia!" I encourage.

"ASS!"

"See?" Caleb says. "I'm not the only one."

"You're so annoying."

He grins down at me. "But you love me."

I can't help the smile I return. "But I love you."

THE END

Psst...

Want more Zoe & Caleb?

Take a look at the sweet note Caleb wrote for Zoe to

celebrate a milestone anniversary...

ZOE,

I can't believe I've spent the last ten years with you.
It's been a wild ride, huh?
From emailing, to being roommates, to you falling
madly in love with me.
Because you are, right? You're madly in love with me?
I'm madly in love with you.
Ten years.
Ten years of bliss.
Ten years of fighting.
Ten years of me teaching you to cook and you almost
burning our house down every time.
Ten years of us.
And somehow, it's still not enough, and I don't think it
ever will be enough.
I love you, Zoe.
And I'm never going to stop.

Happy anniversary, babe.

Always Yours,

CALEB

P.S. In case you're wondering, yes, I did pack those gold
shorts. I can already see you shiver with antici...
...pation

OTHER TITLES BY TEAGAN HUNTER

CAROLINA COMETS SERIES

Puck Shy

Blind Pass

One-Timer

Sin Bin

Scoring Chance

Glove Save

Neutral Zone

ROOMMATE ROMPS SERIES

Loathe Thy Neighbor

Love Thy Neighbor

Crave Thy Neighbor

Tempt Thy Neighbor

SLICE SERIES

A Pizza My Heart

I Knead You Tonight

Doughn't Let Me Go

A Slice of Love

Cheesy on the Eyes

TEXTING SERIES

Let's Get Textual

I Wanna Text You Up

Can't Text This

Text Me Baby One More Time

INTERCONNECTED STANDALONES

We Are the Stars

If You Say So

HERE'S TO SERIES

Here's to Tomorrow

Here's to Yesterday

Here's to Forever: A Novella

Here's to Now

Want to be part of a fun reader group, gain access to exclusive content and giveaways, and get to know me more?

Join Teagan's Tidbits on Facebook!

Want to stay on top of my new releases?

Sign up for New Release Alerts!

ACKNOWLEDGMENTS

To my Marine. Sometimes I cringe when I realize how much you've made it into my books. Every hero I write is you in some way. Then I realize how lucky I am, because every hero I write is pretty fucking amazing. Thank you for ten years of pure craziness. You're my something else, and I wouldn't change a damn thing about that. I love you.

Mom, you're my hero. I don't tell you that enough, but it's true. Thank you for always believing in me. Thanks for always being there despite the distance, and thanks for loving me unconditionally. That's my favorite part about you.

C, Stann, Laurie, and Nikki, thank you *so* much for your notes. Thanks for believing in Caleb and Zoe and for helping me fix that obnoxious FaceTime chapter, and a special shout-out to Stann for "nursing" my book.

As always, my wonderful editor Caitlin with Editing by C. Marie. You push me in the best way possible and I truly feel like my writing has improved because of you. Thank you.

Colleen Hoover, I screenshot all the mean things you say to me. One day I'm going to make a book, and everyone is going to know what an asshole you really are. Kidding...maybe.

My assholes, you know who you are. You're all the worst but in the best way possible.

I have to give Sara Ney a big thank you too. She's always there with her wicked cool accent to answer my random questions or give me advice. You are kind of like the *really* old big sister with amazing eyebrows I never wanted, but I'll never admit that again—like, ever. Douchebag.

#soulmate and Dammit Diann, you two...gah, you just do something to me. Thanks for the best Marco Polo adventures ever.

To my family, by blood and by marriage, your support means everything.

Teagan's Tidbits, we've grown so much over the last few months, and I can't believe how much I've come to rely on you all. You're my rock, my happy place, my special people. Thanks for always being there to participate in my stupid live videos, to creep on the Marine, and to put up with my pizza obsession. It really does mean a lot to me that I have a place where I can just be me and feel accepted and loved. You guys give me that. So, thanks. Okay, enough sappy shit. I don't want Aubrey to think I like her or something.

Readers, thank you for all your support. I cannot believe the enthusiasm that poured in for Delia and Zach when *Let's Get Textual* released. It's still blowing my mind every day. When you guys said you wanted a book for Zoe and Robbie, I panicked because I always knew in my heart that Zoe and Caleb were end game. I was so scared I wasn't going to be able to deliver what you guys wanted, but if you've made it this far and you believe in Zoe and Caleb too, thank you. Thanks for giving me a chance to make you laugh and fall in love with them. I hope you see now why I think they're such a great pair.

With love and unwavering gratitude,
Teagan

TEAGAN HUNTER writes steamy romantic comedies with lots of sarcasm and a side of heart. She loves pizza, hockey, and romance novels, though not in that order. When not writing, you can find her watching entirely too many hours of *Supernatural*, *One Tree Hill*, or *New Girl*. She's mildly obsessed with Halloween and prefers cooler weather. She married her high school sweetheart, and they currently live in the PNW.

www.teaganhunterwrites.com

9 781959 194170